THE REVOLT OF 10-X

THE REVOLT OF 10-X

JOAN DAVENPORT CARRIS

NEW YORK • HARCOURT BRACE JOVANOVICH • LONDON

ACKNOWLEDGMENTS
For assistance with computer information
and knowledge about electrical wiring,
I would like to thank my husband
and Dr. Charles Anderson.

For my family and for Pat

Jacket art by Troy Howell

Requests for permission to make copies of
any part of the work should be mailed to:
Permissions, Harcourt Brace Jovanovich, Inc.,
757 Third Avenue, New York, New York 10017.

Printed in the United States of America

LIBRARY OF CONGRESS CATALOGING IN PUBLICATION DATA
Carris, Joan Davenport.
The revolt of 10X.
SUMMARY: A teenage girl uses a home computer she and her
father built before his death to vent her grief and frustration.
[1. Fathers and daughters—Fiction. 2. Computers—Fiction.
3. Death—Fiction] I. Title.
PZ7.C2347Re   [Fic]   80–7980
ISBN 0-15-266462-9

FIRST EDITION   B C D E

Taylor watched as the last of her bedroom was carted into the new house. It was a dumb house. She hated it. Dumb house, dumb neighborhood. Probably dumb school full of dumb kids.

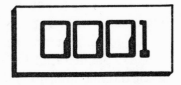

"That's all of it, Mrs. Benson. Sure sorry to hear about your husband." The moving man wiped his sweaty forehead with a red bandanna kerchief. "Hope you'll settle in here real quick. Looks like it's gonna be a nice suburb." He stuffed the red bandanna back into his pocket, waved good-bye, and was gone. The moving van pulled away, and night and the new house were all that was left.

"Taylor?"

"Up here. In this dinky little room in the attic."

Anne Benson sighed. She hadn't wanted to move either. Tiredly she mounted the stairs to Taylor's new bedroom. "Dear, this isn't an attic. I thought you'd like this paneled room at the top of the house. You can pretend you're Jo in *Little Women*—only you have a computer instead of stories to write."

"Big deal." Taylor did not look at her mother as she wheeled the table holding 10-X and its console to the cubby under a dormer window. Taylor bent down and plugged 10-X into the outlet in the wall. The computer, its table, and chair fitted their new slot as if tailor-made.

"See? From your chair you'll be able to see the street and our trees—these are lovely old trees for a new suburb —and work with 10-X at the same time. And 10-X won't blow any fuses here," she added. "The builder assured me this house had the most modern circuitry available. And the best insulation, and—"

"Look, Mother," Taylor interrupted, "I know you want me to be happy here, but you can forget it! I *hate* this house. I don't care how modern it is or how old the stupid trees are! And if you had to go to a new school, you'd understand what I mean."

"Taylor, how many times do we have to go over this? I have explained that I can no longer afford the old house or the old neighborhood. It simply costs too much money. With your sisters grown and gone, we don't need a big house any longer. And you will make new friends. You've always had lots of friends. Why should it be any different now?"

"I don't want new friends! The old ones were fine. I liked them, and they liked me. They say they're going to come to see me, but I know better. In a few weeks they'll forget I'm alive. It'll be just like I moved to Alaska!" Taylor threw herself down on the bed next to her mother.

As her mother smoothed Taylor's dark curls, Taylor buried her head in the pile of bedclothes. Unbidden, the faces of her friends came to mind, laughing, smiling faces —like a parade going away in the distance. One face came and wouldn't leave, the face of her best friend, Karen. Karen had always been there. Always. Together they had learned to walk, to roller skate the uneven sidewalks on Linden Lane, to ride their new bikes.

Stroking her daughter's hair, Anne Benson sighed. If Taylor could cry, her mother thought, she might feel better. The tears were gone, however, shed weeks ago when Jim Benson had died. And Taylor had *always* been her father's girl. Now, her mother realized, all that Taylor had was anger.

Mrs. Benson spoke carefully. "Taylor, new people can become good friends, too." As she spoke, the room was lit by a long flash of white-yellow lightning. Crashing thunder followed and rolled over the house in waves. Rain, soft at first, then driving hard, beat on the roof and western sides of the new house. Mrs. Benson ran downstairs to check the windows. Late-summer storms in Iowa were often welcome, but they'd been known to do some damage.

Taylor went to one of her dormer windows to watch the storm. *The bigger the storm, the better,* she thought. She would watch for the lightning and then count until the crack came. That way she could tell how close the lightning was. There were dozens of flashes, followed by powerful cracks of lightning. Sometimes the two were so close together and so deafening that Taylor thought the house had been struck. The light in her room flickered and went out.

In the dark, she stayed alone at her window and felt the rage of the storm. Up and down the street, houses were dark. Only the lightning illuminated the small cluster of homes.

Taylor groped through the strangeness of her new room to the dresser where she kept her camping flashlight. She lit her way downstairs to the bathroom to brush her teeth and say good-night. It was dark, so she might as well go to bed. There was nothing to do anyway. How dumb everything was now, how terribly dumb and awful. It was fitting that the lights had gone out.

In bed, she asked her lonely question, the one that haunted all her thoughts. *"Where do we go from here?"*

Taylor lay in her bed in the strange new room and dreaded night. Since her father had died, she had learned to hate the night.  Dark thoughts and darker questions came with night. Only three short months ago, one perfectly normal question had been asked in sunlight . . . and her father had been there to answer her.

"Where do we go from here?" Taylor remembered asking. She had tossed the last of her weeds into the bushel basket.

"How about into the house for a nap?" her father had said, grinning. Taylor couldn't forget his grin. In spite of what Professor Benson had termed a crummy job, they had laughed together all that day as they weeded the yard.

The last day, Taylor said to herself. Together they had made the yard a sparkling, carefully tended welcome for her sisters, who were all coming home for the Memorial Day weekend.

"We'll be together for the first time in two whole years," Professor Benson had reminded Taylor as they worked. "Almost makes weeding worthwhile. Whew, it's hot out here! Only one job left, O noble helper, and then we'll go inside and work with 10-X."

"Ha! Don't try to con me with that 'O noble helper' routine! I'm just the only one left who's young enough to *pick* on, that's all."

Her father had chuckled. "It is tough, you know, having only *one pickee!* Take heart! With Brooke and Beth and Whitney here this weekend, I can pick on them and give *you* a break."

"Yeah, I can hardly wait! And Whitney's bringing her newest boyfriend, isn't she?"

Jim Benson had nodded. "Yup. I think we're going to

4

see piles of boyfriends before she picks one and settles down like Brooke and Beth. It's a good thing you girls took after your mother. *She* always had piles of boyfriends, too."

"How could she, with you around?"

"I wasn't always around. I was busy teaching . . . and learning to love computers. That's why we have 10-X, of course, my first love. It's sort of embarrassing to admit you fell in love with computers before you noticed girls." Taylor had laughed. "When I think of what we are going to be able to do with that computer someday! Turn on the sprinkler, run the television, lock the garage . . . you just wait!"

"How about having 10-X do this weeding?" Taylor had asked with a grin.

It's like a movie, Taylor said to herself as she tossed in bed and begged sleep to come. None of it would go away, not one minute, not one word. They had gone into the house that day when the weeding was finished, and they had taken brownies and lemonade up to her large, high-ceilinged bedroom, where 10-X sat.

"We'd better hurry if we're going to finish the surprise for Mother," she had said. "When is the music board coming anyhow? It seems like we've been waiting for it forever."

"It'll come, don't worry. And we'll be ready."

"Are you sure a computer is going to sound like Beethoven?"

"Your mother will *love* it. And we've programmed one of her favorite pieces of music. It's the best surprise idea I've ever had. Even if we have to tie her to the bed for the entire concert!"

"Am I going to understand how to program this music board?"

"Well, we chose fairly simple music this first time, and

even though I'm no expert at it yet, I'd say so. Even a seventh grader ought to figure it out." He had looked innocently at the ceiling.

"Rat! Fink! Don't feed me that stuff about lowly seventh graders!" She had pounded his shoulder, the shoulder that was always next to hers on the piano bench in front of 10-X. "Just for that, no more brownies!"

"I give, I give! Don't pick on me. Remember who's the *pickee* here! Please, *please,* just give me one more brownie. One little nanosecond for one more brownie."

Taylor had shaken her head. "No nanoseconds for brownies. Besides, Karen's coming over tonight, and we're going to make pizza so Mother doesn't have to cook any more. She's cooked all week, getting ready for the big weekend with everybody home, so I said that Karen and I would fix pizza and salad. No more goodies or you'll ruin our special dinner. Anyway, *nobody* could eat a whole brownie in a nanosecond!"

"Want to see somebody try?"

"You can't stay thin and eat brownies, you know."

"You and Karen are always trying to fatten me up. Pizza is fattening!"

"So are brownies!"

"But I'm much more intelligent when I have my weekly ration of brownies. Surely you've noticed that brownies make me smarter."

"What they make you is spoiled." Taylor had given him his brownie anyway, just as she had known she would.

"But I'm so lovable!" Her father had put his arm around Taylor and squeezed.

Taylor knew that as long as she lived, she would remember that feeling of being loved. And miss it.

They had worked the rest of the afternoon with the computer named 10-X. Professor Benson had explained how to program the music for the piece of peripheral equipment that was to come.

6

"I'm certainly glad we saved up and bought this model, Taylor." He had patted 10-X on its broad top. "Some home computers don't adapt as well to extra or peripheral equipment. And not all are as easy to program as this one is."

"Does Mother know that a computer can be programmed to play music?"

"I'm not sure. She may think what we've programmed here isn't music! Well, let's see if we can finish it up before dinner."

Dinnertime had come all too soon, and 10-X was left alone. She and Karen had fixed the pizza and salad, and for once the pizza was a total success.

"This crust is magnificent," Taylor's mother announced. "And I'm awfully fussy about pizza crust. Would you like some more, Jim?"

"No, Anne. Sorry, girls, but I don't seem to be very hungry. I've just tortured this poor salad, and nothing sounds good. You were right, Taylor. Those brownies are bad for me. Guess I'll lie down on the couch awhile."

I should have known, Taylor cried inside. *We all should have known. It was a sign, and we didn't even see it!*

Taylor remembered the rest, all of the rest, every minute of what was left. She and Karen had cleaned up the dinner. They could hear her parents visiting in the living room, anticipating the holiday with all of the girls home together. Professor Benson had talked about his math classes, how they were going, what fun it was to teach computer logic. She and Karen had talked about final exams, looming ahead in the next ten days.

"You'll help me study for the math final, won't you, Taylor?" Karen's tone had been worried.

"Haven't I always? And you can quiz me on Iowa history. I keep mixing up the Indian tribes and where they settled."

"Let's start tonight, okay? Just talking about it makes

7

me *nervous.*" Karen had wadded the dishtowel into a ball and punched it.

They had studied together until almost ten o'clock, and they had tried hard not to talk about anything else. When the front hall clock bonged ten o'clock, Karen had left, clutching the math book and repeating, "*A* equals *pi R* squared. *A* equals *pi R* squared."

The next morning was the really bad time. Taylor and her mother had awakened for the holiday. Everyone in Greensboro had awakened except Jim Benson. During the night he had died. A heart attack, the newspaper was to say the next day. In her mind, Taylor could see the awful words in the obituary column.

Professor James Taylor Benson, of 104 Linden Lane, is survived by his wife, Anne, and daughter Taylor, at home; also by daughters Mrs. Brooke Jeremy of Des Moines, Mrs. Elizabeth Merriam of Chicago, and Miss Whitney Benson of Sioux City. The deceased's sister, Miss Cecilia Benson, also resides in Des Moines.

Interment will be May 31, in Greensboro Memorial Park, at 1 P.M. The family has requested that all gifts in memory be donated to the University Scholarship Fund.

There had been two days before the funeral. Taylor could not talk. She could cry, but she could not talk. What was there to say? What could anyone have said to help? Having Brooke and Beth and Whitney at home hadn't been wonderful at all, because suddenly it was for the wrong reason.

Whitney had stayed close to Taylor the day of the funeral, trying to help by being near. Taylor hadn't been able to talk to Whitney either, even though she'd wanted to.

Now, Taylor thrashed in bed, miserable, hating the dark and its memories. *Where,* she thought, *just where do we go from here?*

By noon the next day, the power knocked out by the storm had been restored to the Bensons' new house. The larger pieces of furniture  were in place, and many of the kitchen boxes had been unpacked. Regretting her temper of the night before, Taylor had spent the morning helping her mother. It was hard work, but it gave them both something to think about. It was part of the new beginning.

When the power came on, they grilled sandwiches for lunch and appreciated electricity all over again.

"Can I go upstairs now?"

"Yes, of course, and thanks for your help. Now that the power's on, you can get 10-X up."

"I suppose." Taylor leaned her chin on her fist. It was hard to even *think* about 10-X, let alone getting it up—making it work once again. 10-X had brought Taylor and her father so close together they'd been like one person. Only now one of them was gone. Sealed up in a dark brown box. Food for worms. Yup, that's what he was.

Taylor remembered her father reading the poem "nobody loses all the time," by a man named Cummings. It was about somebody who messed up everything in life. But when he died, he started a worm farm, sort of, underground. And that was the first successful thing he'd done. Together they'd laughed over the poem, even though her father had said it was really a sad poem.

Oh, yes, Taylor agreed with him silently. *That wasn't funny! Not a bit. Not any more.*

"Well," she said slowly, "school starts in a few weeks, and I'm going to need 10-X." Taylor set her dishes in the sink and stared out the window at their yard. It was running mud from the rain. No grass had been sown in any of the new side or backyards; only a small square of sod graced the front lawns. No flowers bordered the sidewalks as in her old neighborhood in Greensboro. Not even weeds. Just mud.

"We can't have a yard like this! It's icky! They're all icky! I hate these yards!" Taylor shouted at the window.

"Settle down, dear. New suburbs always look like this at first. We wait until the ground firms up and sow grass seed. Early autumn is perfect for sowing grass. Anyway, I love to work outdoors, and it'll give me something to do until I find a job."

"A job? You're going to *work?"* How many changes were there going to be?

"I was under the impression," Mrs. Benson said dryly, "that I'd been working all these years. Now I'll have two jobs so I won't be bored while you're in school. Also, there's the little matter of money. You remember money? As in *allowance?"*

"If you have to work, I couldn't take an allowance. I can mow lawns or baby-sit and earn money myself."

"Taylor, I don't have to work, but I *want* to. I need work to take my mind off old times. I'll enjoy it, is what I'm saying."

"Oh. Well, that's different. I might like earning my allowance too, but first I have to find jobs." *How do you do that in a new neighborhood?* she asked herself.

"Let's get busy and square ourselves away. Tonight we'll eat out to celebrate." Taylor's mother pushed a chair over to the cupboards and climbed up on it to start arranging the shelves.

"Yeah. Celebrate." Taylor dragged upstairs to her room. The room was just as it had been the night before, a mess. Lampshades waited in boxes; books waited in boxes; all of her collections for thirteen years waited in boxes. "Poop on it!" She kicked some of the boxes into a corner and sat down at the computer console.

10-X looked at Taylor in silence. Taylor stared at the computer she and her father had loved and felt the terrible pain again. Maybe she should destroy 10-X, and then all the memories would go away. She wouldn't see her father's hands on the keyboard or hear his voice explaining all the things a computer could do . . . turn on the sprinkler, lock the garage. She covered her face with her hands. If 10-X were gone, it couldn't make her feel this way ever again.

She reached under the table for the box of tools, her father's box of tools that had built the computer. The little hammer would do it. It would be slow, but satisfying. She could pound the entire computer into tiny bits. Then she could smash the bits.

Taylor raised the hammer and told herself to do it. *Beat on it. Pound on it.* The hammer was steady in her hand. *Wreck it!* She held the hammer poised over the machine and took a deep breath. And another breath. "Oh, dammit!" She dropped the hammer to the floor and leaned her head on 10-X. She couldn't do it. This *thing* was all she had, all that remained of James Taylor Benson. Curse it, hate it, it was still all there was.

Once there had been a tall, straight man with dark hair. A person who had said, "You'll never be too big to sit on my lap, punkin. Being a math teacher is my disguise, you know. Actually I'm a professional father. That's my favorite job. It pays the best, too. All the university ever gives me is money. My daughters pay me with hugs and kisses. Now I ask you?" And then he would laugh. He could make anyone laugh. Jim Benson had been tall in more than feet and inches. No wonder his classes had been jammed with students. No wonder she missed him.

Taylor swore again and kicked the hammer across the room. She looked back at 10-X and, after a long time, let out a big sigh. Her father would want her to enjoy this thing they had built together. Why was it so hard? And when was it going to get better?

In the meantime, here was 10-X—dusty, dirty, and

down. A computer that was down, not running, was no good to anyone. Memories or not, she couldn't wreck it. Not now, not ever. Instead, she cleaned it, wiping until every inch shone. She dug out her instruction booklet to check the wiring. After several adjustments she was satisfied. 10-X would come up. It would run again. Everything else, absolutely everything else had changed, but not 10-X. At least there was that.

The joy of Taylor's computer was its ability to take instructions in a language close to English. The machine's compiler program converted the program language Taylor and her father had made up into machine language. 10-X would crunch away on the problem in machine language and convert its answer to their program language. Then the results would appear on the screen.

BEBOP, keyed Taylor. It was her code name, a password. Professor Benson had been Bop. At large computer installations, each user had to have a password. Taylor's father had thought their passwords a good joke.

HALLELUJAH! GIVE ME A JOB.

NO. ALL BEBOP SYSTEMS DOWN, Taylor typed. There was a pause while 10-X digested this unusual reply.

EXPLAIN, was the best 10-X could muster.

LIFE HAS BOMBED, typed Taylor.

As she punched "bombed" on the keyboard, she noticed a sudden stillness in the house. Taylor walked to the head of the stairs and listened carefully. She strained to hear the comforting tick-tock of their old hall clock— *nothing*—only the hum of her computer. Then she heard her mother's exasperated voice.

"Just look at that! It's stopped. Everything's stopped! Now I don't need this."

Taylor heard her mother waggling wall switches, muttering about builder's claims for modern wiring and the awful heat. "Taylor?"

"Yes, Mother?"

"Did you do anything funny up there? Are your lights on?"

"No. And yes, my light is on." Taylor frowned, thinking. She left 10-X and went downstairs to see and hear for herself.

"Darn it anyway!" said Mrs. Benson as Taylor came into the kitchen. Her mother pushed damp strands of hair out of her eyes and made a face at the fan. "There's no electricity down here, and so I have no fan, no vacuum, no refrigerator—no anything! I wonder if the main transformer is out because of that storm?" She marched to the phone to call the power company.

While her mother spoke with the service representative at the power company, Taylor's mind whirled. She remembered the blinding flashes of the storm's lightning —the incredibly swift-following cracks. Maybe there *was* something funny going on. Certainly the wiring was different from their old house in Greensboro, where even two appliances could blow a fuse. Yes, there was something different.

Maybe it was a *glitch.*

Taylor sat in front of 10-X, frozen in thought. *A glitch.* Did glitches really happen, or were they another of her father's jokes?

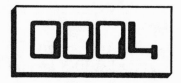

"What do you mean your office computer's down because of a glitch?" she had asked her father. *"You're putting me on again, toad! Seeing if I read up on those terms or not, huh? Aren't you?"*

Jim Benson had grinned. *"Not this time, sweetheart, believe me. It's a freak happening, but glitch is a good slang term to describe it. A glitch describes electrical circuits that are acting up, misbehaving, sort of. Sometimes glitches are triggered by electrical noise, like a big storm near by. Honest! Would I kid around when my very own computer is down?"*

Hmmph. Taylor was still skeptical. But they had certainly been in a big storm. And very near by. She'd felt as if the house had been hit once or twice.

"Maybe. Maybe it is a glitch," she said out loud. Just for the heck of it, she typed 100%. It was a code word meaning "perfect" or "stupendous." A compliment to the computer it was. Another of Jim Benson's jokes.

Upon reading 100%, the computer reacted. THANK YOU. IT WAS NOTHING. Now Taylor heard the vacuum cleaner rev into action downstairs in the kitchen. She strained to hear more and was rewarded with a burp from the noisy refrigerator motor. The fan whirred, and even the hall clock ticked and tocked. Mrs. Benson's voice rose above everything as she wondered aloud about the power company.

Taylor leaned back in her chair, amazed. When she'd keyed "bombed," the downstairs electricity had gone off at the same time. Was that a coincidence? "100%" had been a lucky guess, she was sure of that, but the electricity *had* come on again. *"Weird,"* she said out loud. Maybe

14

it was just a fluke. Maybe "bombed" hadn't triggered the shutoff.

But suppose the word "bomb" or "bombed" did control the electricity in the new house?

"Taylor? Let's clean up and go out to dinner," Mrs. Benson called from the foot of the stairs. "I'm not going to peek in on you, but I'll bet you've done a lot of work up there, too, right?"

Taylor looked around guiltily. *Not exactly, Mother,* she mumbled to herself. *Not so's you'd notice.* "Well," she compromised out loud, "at least 10-X is in order."

"What's that, dear? I couldn't hear you."

"I said 10-X is up and working fine. I'll change clothes and be right down." Taylor turned the switch that shut off the computer. In the wardrobe box, waiting to be unpacked like everything else, she found a denim skirt and a striped summer top. All the time she dressed, she eyed her computer. It had been an interesting afternoon. *Very* interesting.

Mrs. Benson felt comfortably relaxed as they sat in the restaurant later having dinner. Taylor was preoccupied, but pleasant.

"So, if I take all the math I can get in high school, maybe I can win a scholarship to major in computer science at the university."

Mrs. Benson started to say how proud she was of such a goal but was interrupted by a decidedly *round* little man.

"Pardon me. Couldn't help overhearing your talk during dinner. I'm George Stout, and we live just down the street from you folks. We heard you were moving in this week and were tickled pink, Mama and I, because our little gal's been awfully lonesome out here in Kingswood Manor. No kids yet, you see. Too new, I guess. Anyway, you two'll have to get together." He paused to beam at Taylor. "So I said to myself, why not *now?*"

Mr. Stout took a hasty breath and went on, "Anastasia! You and Mama come over here," he called loudly. Everyone in the restaurant turned to look at the Bensons' table. Taylor blushed and looked down at her plate. *Anastasia? Anastasia Stout?*

"Hi," said Anastasia Stout.

Taylor looked up, but not too far. Anastasia was short, like her father. And round, like her father. She looked about nine.

"Hello. I'm Taylor Benson. It's nice to meet you." It was a terribly polite little speech.

"Thanks. Are you going to the junior high in September? I'm going to be in the eighth grade."

Taylor started to say that she too was an eighth grader, but Mr. Stout leaped into the conversation.

"Smartest little gal in all Iowa! Took those big tests and went right off the chart! Mama and I couldn't get over it. We put all our eggs in one basket, heh-heh, but she's one heck of a basket! Right, Mama?"

"Right, dear." Mrs. Stout smiled nervously, as if she wished Mr. Stout would be quiet, and greeted Taylor's mother. Mrs. Stout was about half as tall as Mrs. Benson. Taylor wondered if she were a midget. She was round, too, but not nearly so round as her husband and daughter.

"Won't you come back to the house?" Taylor heard her mother say. "I have a cake in the freezer, and if I can remember where I put the coffeepot, we'll have coffee."

"Now, Mrs. Benson, that's our pleasure, welcoming you to the neighborhood. I have homemade cherry pie cooling on the counter. You folks just come to our place. We're in the blue house on the corner. It's Number Ten, with a yellow door."

In the car, Taylor brooded. She wanted to spend the evening in her room testing 10-X. The last thing she wanted to do was visit Anastasia Stout. If she was so all-fired smart, she'd probably skipped several grades and really was nine years old!

"How long do we have to stay?"

"I'm sorry, Taylor, but it is important for us to get to know the families in the neighborhood. Besides, the Stouts seem good-hearted, and I think I'll like 'Mama' when I get to know her. I hope she has another name." Mrs. Benson laughed.

"Yeah. And Anastasia! Can you believe that?"

In no time at all, the Bensons had driven home and put the car in the garage. Taylor slumped down the street after her mother to the Stouts' house. She thought of all the names Mrs. Stout could have. While her mother rang the doorbell, Taylor was betting on *Euphemia*.

"Come right in. George is making his special after-dinner coffee for us. Anastasia? Your guest is here. Just go on back to the kitchen, Taylor. The 'old folks' will visit in the living room."

Across the kitchen table Taylor and Anastasia looked awkwardly at one another. Anastasia spoke first.

"It was the milkman who told us you'd moved in. He said your dad died last spring. You can share mine if you want. Daddy turns people off at first, because he gets all excited meeting new folks, especially city people. But you'll love him when you get to know him. And he has enough love for forty daughters." She looked earnestly at Taylor.

Taylor didn't know what to say. One part of her was amazed at the warmth of such an offer. The other part was outraged. The idea of George Stout as a replacement father was ridiculous. Her father had been tall and slender and witty and educated.

"Don't say anything now, about Daddy, I mean. I didn't say it very well anyhow. Don't you want to know what my mother's name is after hearing mine?"

Grateful for a different subject, Taylor nodded. "It's Chloe."

"*Clowee?* How do you spell it?"

"C-h-l-o-e. Weird, isn't it? It's Greek. Supposed to mean young and green, or an herb, something like that. She hates it, so she gave me a *pretty* name."

"Oh." Taylor was nonplussed.

"It helps if I laugh about it." Anastasia grinned, and then Taylor felt comfortable about smiling back. It was pretty funny when you thought about it. Still, she was glad it wasn't *her* name.

"What I need is a nickname," Anastasia said firmly. "Mama told all the teachers in my old school to call me Anastasia, and it stuck. Like glue." Her face was as long as a round face can get.

"How about Stacy? You look kind of like a Stacy." Taylor examined her for the first time. Anastasia was pretty, even though she was quite round. Her eyes were large and wonderfully green, like stones in a jeweler's window. Her hair was the color of sand with sun on it; her smile, hard to resist. She had perfect skin. Too bad she was built like a basketball.

"Stacy? Yeah, I like it. Only Stacys are thin. *I* am fat, as you can see. And I look like a little kid."

Surprised into helpfulness, Taylor volunteered, "But you'd look older if you were thinner."

"I've tried. Diet foods are crummy. One year I ate apples all the time, just to lose weight. Then I found out that a big apple has about a hundred calories. And they're gassy. I gained five pounds that year and lived in the bathroom besides. It was awful."

Taylor laughed. Anastasia-or-Stacy *was* funny. She wouldn't have any trouble making friends at the new school. "Sometime," Taylor offered, "I could have 10-X plan a diet for you, if you want. 10-X is my computer. My father and I built it from a kit."

"Your very own computer?"

"Yes." *Now* it was her very own.

"When? Can you show me how it works? Would it tell me not to eat this pie?" Stacy licked her fork appreciatively. "Will it be heartless and mean?"

"Computers don't have feelings. But I can't do it for you now. Maybe after school starts we could write a program for diet meals." *First,* she said to herself, *I need to know more about glitches.*

Stacy set her plate in the sink with a loud clank. "I can start on my own, I guess. But if I can't eat, I have to be busy. Let's go out to the garage and I'll give you something. That'll keep us busy."

Taylor rose from the table hesitantly. Give her something? What could Stacy have in the garage that she would want?

Taylor followed Stacy out the back door and down the short driveway to the Stouts' garage. "Give me something?" she said to Stacy.

"Surprise," Stacy tossed back over her shoulder. "You'll love it." She opened the door a crack. "Here. Take this stick. You'll need it for Honker. Honker hates strangers." She handed a long, thick stick to Taylor.

"Honker?"

Both girls stepped into the dimness that was the Stouts' garage. Immediately a large bluish gray shape flew across the cement floor, wings flapping, beak honking.

"Use the stick! Wave it around in front of you! Honker's afraid of sticks."

"I'm afraid of Honker!" Taylor squeaked. She slashed the air with her stick, and Honker subsided into hisses. He juked his white head up and down and hissed as the girls stood still and let him adjust to their presence. "What is he exactly?" Taylor asked, her calmness returning.

"A blue goose. So's Sally, his wife, and all their babies. The babies are only a couple weeks old. You'll like them better. Better than Honker, I mean. Just stand still for a few more minutes."

"Gotcha. How many geese are in here anyway?"

"Too many, that's how many. We have roast goose at Thanksgiving and Christmas and Easter, which helps, but Sally keeps hatching new ones. We're going to eat the rest of the teenagers this year, but I don't know what we'll do with these new ones."

"Eat them? Geese you *know?*"

"Farmers never think about that. We had to move away from our farm. That's why we're living in town now. Daddy has a bad heart, so he's managing a bunch of farms for other people. Sally and Honker were my pets, so we brought their family with us."

Taylor nodded, understanding. So, she wasn't the only one in Kingswood Manor whose life had changed. Too bad she and Stacy didn't have more in common.

"Let's go see the babies. Sally likes to have folks admire her family." Stacy beckoned to Taylor, and both moved slowly toward the back of the garage, where Sally rested on a pile of hay. Taylor waved the stick in Honker's direction and bent down to look at the goslings. She'd had pets, but they'd been gerbils and guinea pigs. She'd never thought of a goose as a pet. Did geese make good pets?

Peeping and peering one-eyed at the newcomer, the goslings crowded around her, and Taylor was drawn to them in spite of herself. "They're cute," she said, stroking the soft down on the babies.

"Cute-ugly. But I have fun with them. They follow me all around the yard in a line, just like I'm their mother. Blue geese are pretty smart. At least Sally is. I've never been too sure about Honker."

Taylor petted the geese, one especially, who nuzzled her hand repeatedly. It was the smallest of the babies.

"Is that the one you want?"

"Want? To keep, you mean?"

"Sure. That way yours wouldn't get eaten. It could live in your garage, and we could build a pond for it, like I did for mine. Go on, pick one out. I haven't named any of them yet."

Again Taylor's hand smoothed the down on the smallest baby. A goose for a pet? A goose was probably better than a gerbil. "Thanks. How about this darker one? It's so small, maybe nobody would want it except me. Would your mother get upset if I named it Chloe?"

"No, but she'd suggest a pretty name like Clotilde or Minerva or Eulalia instead." Stacy made a face.

"Where does she dream up names like that?"

"More important, *why* does she? Go on, hold her in

21

your hand and let her get used to you."

Taylor picked up the tiny gosling and felt it nestle into her palm. It cocked its head and examined her with one bright eye. Then it peep-peeped a greeting. That did it. Chloe was adopted.

"You can't take her yet, but in a few days she'll be old enough—if you stay with her. Geese need lots of company. Wish I could get rid of the others as easy as this."

"Couldn't you put up a sign in school this fall? It'd be a good way to meet kids."

"Yeah! Town kids would love a country-type pet. But how about town *mothers?*"

"I don't think mine will care. Let's show her Chloe and ask."

That evening, in the living room of the Stouts' house, with George Stout's special company coffee, the gosling was christened: Chloe Minerva Benson. Taylor asked that Anastasia be christened Stacy at the same time. Although Mama Stout protested, George Stout agreed with Taylor. He said the name Stacy was "with it." After the two christenings, Chloe was tucked under her mother's wing to grow up a bit. The Bensons said their thanks and went back to the new house.

Later Taylor lay in bed stiffly, trying to feel at home in the strange room with the peaked ceiling. She had wanted to test "bomb" on 10-X again to see what happened, but there was so little electrical noise that she wouldn't get a quick answer. She'd have to find out tomorrow.

Hurrying to get to sleep so that tomorrow would come, Taylor thought about Stacy. And Chloe. But they both were so new and so different that it was hard to feel comfortable with them. She wanted to, but she couldn't. Not yet. Maybe tomorrow. Maybe tomorrow she could call Karen and have her come for a visit. Being with Karen had always been comfortable. As babies she and

Karen had been pushed in carriages up and down Linden Lane. Linden Lane.

Taylor buried her head in her pillow to blot out the picture of the house and neighborhood she loved. Why didn't tomorrow hurry up and come?

Taylor woke up to hear her mother in the kitchen. Mrs. Benson was running the small electric mixer. *Yum, yum,* Taylor thought. *That*  *means pancakes.* She remembered that it also meant electrical noise. For a second she hesitated, looking from her bed across the room to 10-X. Then she leaped up and ran to test her theory.

BEBOP.

HALLELUJAH! GIVE ME A JOB.

BOMB, Taylor typed decisively. She sat still, listening.

"Well, really!" Taylor heard her mother's disbelieving voice. "Not again!" There was a sound of jiggling electrical switches. "I hope they get things sorted out down at that power company!"

Upstairs, Taylor sat at the computer and gazed ahead in amazement. *How could it be? Could a glitch foul up the circuitry so that it was controlled by one electrical appliance like a computer?* Surely it was a rare thing, a very rare thing. But there wasn't much doubt any longer. Was there? Briefly, Taylor wondered about the supermodern wiring in the house that the builder had bragged about.

100%. She heard the mixer whip into action, and her mother's frustrated moan reached her ears.

"Blew the danged batter all over the place! Good morning to me," Mrs. Benson sang humorlessly.

THANK YOU. IT WAS NOTHING, replied 10-X.

"Well, what do you know about that?" Taylor said softly. She turned off the computer and began dressing. 10-X could control the new house. No, that wasn't right. She controlled 10-X, so *she* controlled the new house.

But she didn't want to control the new house! She didn't want anything to do with it. It was a dumb house, and she hated it. Perhaps, though, it might come in handy to be running the house's electricity. If she had to vacuum, and

24

the vacuum were temporarily "broken," it would be handy for sure. If 10-X made life absolutely *awful* in the new house, they might not have to stay. Their old house wasn't sold yet. They could go home again.

"No, dummy!" she said aloud. "You know better. We can't go back because Mother said we can't afford to live there any more."

But Mother had changed her mind other times. Why not this time? Mother was the one who was always saying that people who were afraid to change their minds just weren't thinking. She said being strong enough to change your mind was a sign of intelligence.

"Taylor? Come on down to breakfast. I made pancakes. It was a struggle, but I did it!" A low laugh reached the upstairs.

Taylor listened and was forced to admire her mother's determination. *She can even laugh,* Taylor thought. "Be right down," she called. She finished putting on yesterday's old clothes. No need to dress up. Today she was going to hibernate with 10-X. She'd make a code—a code of words that would run the entire house from upstairs in her bedroom!

"Mother," Taylor asked at breakfast, "do you like it here?"

"Yes, I think so, but it's too soon to tell. As soon as I've met other people on the block and am busy with a job, I imagine I'll settle in and be quite comfortable. At least that's the plan I'm working on."

"But it can never be like living on Linden Lane? It could never be as good as that!"

Mrs. Benson looked sad. "No, probably not. Nothing will ever be exactly like that again. But I want to try to look ahead, not back. That hurts too much."

Taylor nodded. "So you think this helps to look ahead, this moving to a new place? Couldn't you have worked at a job and stayed in Greensboro?" Taylor hoped hard, silently.

Her mother nodded. "Perhaps. A job would have helped certainly, but I can't say for sure. I can't say that this move is the perfect answer either. Maybe I reacted too quickly, as Aunt Cissy tells me." Her face closed, and she said no more.

"Aunt Cissy! Is she butting in again?"

"Taylor! That's not nice and you know it. Aunt Cissy regards us as her family. After all, she practically raised your father after their mother died, and she cares for all of us very much."

"Maybe so, but she just makes me *furious.* Every time she comes for a visit she tells everybody what to do, when to do it, what to say. She never quits!"

"I know," her mother agreed wearily. "She's on duty again, too. She called this morning and woke me up to say that she's coming to see how we're settling in. I tell myself she means well, but it's still hard to take."

Taylor chewed her pancakes and fumed. Aunt Cissy. She really didn't want to see Aunt Cissy ever again until she was older and could say some of the things she felt! Out loud. Somebody was going to have to tell Aunt Cissy off *sometime!*

"I don't *want* her to come, at least not now, Mother. You said I could have Karen come to visit. Let's have Karen first. That's a lot more fun."

"I agree. Don't tell Aunt Cissy that, but I agree. However, it is Aunt Cissy who called and Aunt Cissy who's coming, like it or not. As soon as she's gone, you can have Karen for a visit."

Taylor stabbed another pancake from the serving plate. Well, now she *did* have her work cut out for her. 10-X was going to control the house, all right, and in time for Aunt Cissy's visit. Life was going to be *just rotten* in the new house. If Aunt Cissy couldn't stand it, then she'd leave in

a hurry and Karen could come. Taylor smiled o̶
window.

All day, while Mrs. Benson unpacked boxes in t̶
downstairs bedrooms and hung draperies in the living
room, Taylor and 10-X worked on the house circuits.
Amazing things began to appear on Taylor's note pad. By
the end of the afternoon the note pad said:

BOMB—everything off, except my room
100%—everything on again
SUNSET—west wall circuits off. In kitchen, no toaster & no
light over table. Hot-water heater off in the basement. Bath off.
West wall off in Mother's room.
STORM—north wall circuits off in guest room. One outside
wall off in Mother's room.
GARBAGE—south wall switches off in living room. (TV
plug?) Sink light in kitchen off.

Not bad, Taylor mused as she reread the note pad. A
good beginning.
100%.
THANK YOU. IT WAS NOTHING.
She flopped on her bed to relax. There'd been dozens of
trips up and down stairs to check out her code. In order
to test the various light plugs, she had had to carry her
little radio around the house to see if it worked when
plugged in. The trips to the basement had meant feeding
some very flimsy excuses to her mother. Hundreds of
wrong guesses had made her temper flare. Furiously she
had typed "Garbage!" That was how she'd found the clue
to the plug on the south wall. It had been a trying day. But
now that there were several words in the code, the idea of
controlling the house was more exciting than ever.
Taylor filed the precious notebook under her mattress
for safekeeping. She didn't know what kind of trouble she
could dream up, but it was going to be interesting. Some-

body was finally going to be able to put Aunt Cissy in her place. And maybe, just maybe, she could change her mother's mind about living in the new house.

Night and bedtime came again. Taylor tossed uncomfortably and hated night. Why was it so hard? Why did she always think about her father when she was alone in the dark? Bop, the worm farm—what an awful thought. She supposed her mother had bad thoughts, too. Well, she and 10-X could give everybody something new to think about. Any time now.

As soon as possible the next day Taylor sat down to work with 10-X again. She had been working only a few minutes when her mother  called up the stairs. "Taylor? Stacy's here. She can come upstairs, can't she?"

Taylor groaned. Stacy was a nice enough person, but Taylor had work to do, and she didn't want anybody hanging around, asking questions. Stacy would be sure to ask questions.

"Taylor? Did you hear me?"

"I heard you."

Downstairs, Stacy heard also, especially Taylor's tone of voice. "It's okay, Mrs. Benson. I can come another time when she isn't busy. It's just such a beautiful day I thought we could take a walk or something."

Taylor listened and felt mean. "It's okay," she called down the stairs. "But I'm still a mess up here."

"I don't care. I can help unpack if you want. It's just so boring at my house. Ooh," said Stacy admiringly when she reached Taylor's room, "this paneling's pretty. How'd you get this neat room? My folks said we had to keep our upstairs room for company, so I'm in the other downstairs bedroom at our house. I just *love* this wood paneling. Like having your very own cabin."

"I suppose I'll get used to it."

Stacy heard again, words that Taylor had not said. Tactfully she changed the subject. "Is that 10-X or whatever you call him?"

"Computers are *it's* not *he's*. They don't have personalities."

"Mine would. Especially if it could do all my math homework. Anything that could do that would have the finest personality in the whole world!"

Taylor smiled. That was how Karen had felt about 10-X's ability to do math.

"Well? Could it do that? Do my math homework?"

"Sure. It just does what you and I do, only faster. Lots faster."

"Good. I'll be in second-year Latin, and that's easy—everything's easy—but math stinks! I can add and subtract, and that's it."

"That's what 10-X does. Multiplication is just a lot of addition, and division is just quick subtraction."

"How's come you know that stuff and I don't?" wailed Stacy.

"My father."

Stacy was silent. She hadn't meant to be a reminder. "Guess I'll run along. You look pretty busy. Little Chloe's doing just fine. I'll keep an eye on her for you and let you know now and then, okay?" Stacy edged toward the stairs.

"Sure. And thanks, thanks a lot." Taylor smiled as warmly as she could. Sometime soon she'd have time for Stacy, but not now, she thought, not when she had to do such an important job.

Taylor listened as Stacy said good-bye to Mrs. Benson. Stacy had such a clear voice that Taylor couldn't help overhearing.

"It's okay, Mrs. Benson, really. I understand. A couple years ago Mama lost another baby, must be three or four by now, and we had a bad time for months. Mama wouldn't go out or do anything, but Daddy said that wasn't right, and he made her get into things again. I understand how it is, really I do, and it'll be all right after a while. We just have to be patient."

Mrs. Benson, unseen by Taylor, hugged Stacy. She dropped a few tears on Stacy's sandy hair. But that was all right. Stacy understood. "Come back soon, Stacy. I mean that."

Taylor listened as the door shut behind Stacy. She

should have been nicer, she decided, since Stacy was so nice. But then, it was easy for her. *She* hadn't lost *her* father. George Stout wasn't Taylor's idea of the perfect father, but he was Stacy's, and she still had him around. Whenever she wanted him.

Chloe would be good company, Taylor reminded herself. Yes, Chloe would be a perfect friend. She wouldn't expect Taylor to be nice all the time, and she wouldn't ask questions. When Taylor got bored with her, she could put her in her cage. A pet was good that way. It liked you no matter what.

Taylor turned back to 10-X. Electricity was a powerful tool. If she kept her promise to Stacy, then Stacy would soon be eating only what an electric appliance told her to eat if she wanted to lose weight.

"That's a good way to find words!" Taylor got out her instruction book and read again about writing programs. She would write a program for diet menus and give 10-X food-calorie information. Menus would print out on the screen, and maybe some of those words would trigger the house electrical outlets. Taylor ran downstairs for the calorie books that had belonged to Whitney. She found them in *The Chocolate Cookbook*. Like her father, Whitney was mad about chocolate, and all of her diets had included a chocolate reward at the end of the day. Taylor smiled, remembering Whitney's determination to diet and remain happy about it. She'd have to keep a few goodies in Stacy's diet, too.

Several hours passed as Taylor patiently worked on a program that would print out menus of 1,000 calories a day. Dozens of new words were put into 10-X's memory bank. When she finished the program, she began testing to see if any of the new combinations of letters would trigger the house circuits. Electricity, her father had said, was really a simple thing. A switch waited for certain voltage pulses to come along; then it reacted accordingly, turning on or off. Taylor knew that her code words, if they were right, would cause the computer to radiate impulses through the power lines to the switches.

Again Taylor tested outlets with her radio. She moved quickly, knowing that her mother would quit work in the yard and come in to fix dinner before long. None of the new letter combinations turned off any of the wall outlets, and Taylor knew it would take luck as well as perseverance to find the right words. As her mother came in the kitchen door, Taylor hurried upstairs with her radio.

"Would you like to walk down to Stout's this evening?" Mrs. Benson asked hopefully. She wiped the counter as Taylor folded the tablecloth.

"No, thanks. I'm reading a good book. You go, though. You need to get away."

"If I stay here, I'll work! It's a disease. I'd rather have you with me, though. . . ." She waited.

"I'm fine. Don't worry about me, okay?" Taylor smiled to reassure her mother.

The minute the door closed behind her, Taylor zipped upstairs to get the radio and key in a new word for testing. How lucky that Mrs. Stout was such a nice person. Maybe her mother would spend a lot of time there, and time was all Taylor needed.

Time worked in Taylor's favor. In the next few days Mrs. Benson put many hours into the yard work she loved. She also visited the Stouts frequently, finding a warm and understanding friend in Mama Stout. Taylor, on the other hand, found several new words to add to the list in the note pad. As she and her radio moved methodically around the house, her list grew in power. Eventually each circuit on the main floor and in the basement was tagged with a word that would turn it off. These code words were written on the note pad:

MEDIAN—east wall of kitchen off. This means re.
and stove. Also, one inside wall in Mother's room.
CENTER—furnace off (basement). "Sunset" for west base.
wall? "Daylight" for east basement wall?
DAYLIGHT—East wall in guest room. Front wall of livin.
room, and porch light, too.

Her favorite discovery was "fowl." Whenever "fowl" was
keyed in, the south wall plug in the living room went off,
as did the utility plug directly below it in the basement.
The television set was plugged in at that wall outlet in the
back corner of the living room. Aunt Cissy, due to arrive
any time, was addicted to television, even the daytime
programs. Taylor could hardly wait to "fowl" up the television set.

The morning of Aunt Cissy's arrival Taylor was upstairs at work with 10-X when she stumbled on the best
word of all. Downstairs, the vacuum cleaner was gobbling
up the yard dirt tracked in all week long by Mrs. Benson.
SUPER! keyed Taylor. It was an end word, part of
their regular programming language.
"Ye gods!" shrieked Mrs. Benson. The vacuum revved
its motor until smoke poured out from its base. Then it
stopped, still smoking. Mrs. Benson yanked the cord from
its wall plug. Taylor pelted downstairs to see what had
happened.
"Wow! What went wrong?"
"I'm sure I don't know! Either this thing works itself to
death, like now, or it won't work at all! Now I'll have to
get it repaired or buy a new one, and we can't afford either.
I'd better forget the yard and find a job. Our budget's
squeaking to get the old washer and dryer repaired, and
now this." Mrs. Benson sat down in a chair and rubbed
her forehead nervously.
"I'll borrow Stout's since we're getting ready for company. I'll even finish the vacuuming." Taylor patted her

other's shoulder and set off for Stacy's house.

Her mind and feet raced. Something had caused the vacuum's motor to go berserk. That something almost *had* to be 10-X. And the word had to be "super." That storm had thoroughly jinxed the circuits to the new house. Not for the first time, Taylor wondered about the circuitry in the new house. If the builder ever came around, she'd have to ask him about it. Meanwhile, though, she was in a quandary. Would "super" send extra voltage to any outlet and overload the circuit, or just to that one outlet? Was it 10-X for sure, or just a wiring mistake? If other outlets were overloaded, other appliances would be messed up. That would make life in the new house absolutely miserable, wouldn't it?

But is that what I want? Taylor asked herself. *Will it help?* Taylor slowed to a walk, mind and feet taking time out.

The old, wounded vacuum cleaner had been bundled off to the back hall and the Stouts' loaner returned before Aunt Cissy arrived. The 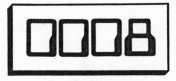 Bensons' new house was in order. Mrs. Benson and Taylor had called the Benson girls, Brooke, Beth, and Whitney, to tell them they were all settled and expecting company.

"Aunt Cissy?" moaned Beth over the phone. "Remember the time I was away at camp and she talked you and Dad into painting my room bright yellow? She *knew* I hated yellow! I've never forgiven her for that. Now, Mother, don't you let her get you down. And, Taylor?"

"Yeah, I'm on in Mother's room."

"Taylor, you just stick to your guns. Go for a lot of walks. And take Mother with you!"

Taylor laughed. "It's okay, Beth. I don't think she'll stay very long." She smiled to herself, the smile weakening as she thought how her father would regard her plans. Aunt Cissy was a topic they had argued about several times, she remembered.

Later Mrs. Benson finished hanging the watercolors in the living room and stepped back to admire the effect. Pillows were flopped comfortably in chairs, and rows of books stood on their shelves in the living room and hallway.

"I declare, Anne, it looks as though you've been here a month," Aunt Cissy announced as she strode in the doorway. "I'll help you straighten those watercolors in the morning. Tonight there's a program on television that I always watch. That's why I drove down right after work and a quick supper to be in time for my program."

Mrs. Benson nodded and repressed a smile. "So you're still doing typing at home? Well, it was thoughtful of you to take the time to come and see us. How about a cup of tea after that long drive? The kitchen's back here. Those steps lead up to Taylor's room. Taylor? Your aunt's here," called Mrs. Benson as the two women proceeded into the kitchen.

"Hi, Aunt Cissy," said Taylor as she joined them in the kitchen.

"Hello, dear. How's it going here? Have you made a lot of new friends? Don't pick at your fingernails, Taylor. Ladies never have ragged fingernails. Have you seen your new school yet? Are there any nice-looking boys on this street? Don't you love this new house?" Aunt Cissy reached over to pat Taylor on the arm.

Taylor winced. "No," she answered to everything. "And I'll see the new school soon enough."

Anne Benson spoke quickly, aware that Aunt Cissy had touched every raw nerve in one short speech. "Cissy, come outside with me for a minute before it's too dark to see anything. The yard here is going to be a real treasure. I've started a rose bed, and the soil is marvelous." Firmly she led Cissy outdoors before there was any more unpleasantness.

Taylor watched them go outside and made up her mind, not that there had been much doubt. One day of Aunt Cissy would be more than enough. Taylor tramped upstairs to 10-X.

BEBOP.
HALLELUJAH! GIVE ME A JOB.
DAYLIGHT.

"Taylor, dear?" It was Aunt Cissy calling. "Come down and keep me company while I unpack, and bring your yearbook for me to see. Your mother said you had several good pictures in it this year."

Taylor poked through boxes, hunting for her yearbook. *Yes, Aunt Cissy,* she said to herself as she jumped down the steps. *With pleasure, Aunt Cissy. May your teeth rot in their glass, Aunt Cissy.*

"Now. You just sit there on the bed and tell me all about this place. The area's full of new homes, so there must be lots of teenagers. Am I right?" Aunt Cissy fiddled with the lamp switch. "Turn on the wall switch, Taylor. I can't get this lamp to work."

Taylor turned the switch to On. Nothing happened.

"Goodness, we have to have electricity! It's chilly tonight, and the furnace may have to come on." Aunt Cissy nervously rubbed her hands together. "Anne? I think you've a bulb burned out here in the guest room; at least that's what I hope. Give Taylor a new one, all right?"

Taylor carried the new bulb into the guest room, and Aunt Cissy exchanged bulbs. She switched the lamp on, but it stayed off. "Turn that wall switch to Off, Taylor. Maybe the builder got confused the day he installed switches in this room." Taylor obediently turned the wall switch to Off.

"Anne? This lamp won't work. I'll have to have another one. I'm determined to unpack before my program."

A substitute lamp was unearthed from boxes in the basement, and the process started all over. Two light bulbs later, Aunt Cissy said, "Plug this lamp into that socket on the other side of the room, and just set it on the floor. I have to be able to *see* in here at night."

"Sure, Aunt Cissy, only let me run upstairs first and turn off my curling iron. I was doing my hair when you came and I think I left it on. Hate to burn down the new house, ha-ha," joked Taylor. She bolted out of the room.

STORM, typed Taylor, smiling at the video screen. As long as she could make up good excuses, she could run up and down all she liked. This was fun, she thought as she ran back downstairs.

"Okay. Here goes. On with the light," announced Taylor as she plugged the lamp into the socket. Nothing happened.

"My stars, but this is aggravating! I'll want an electric

37

blanket for this cold, and what will we do without electricity in here?" Again Aunt Cissy rubbed her hands together. "Well, I guess I'll leave the suitcase till morning. I always read in bed, too, before I go to sleep. *But not tonight,*" she added grimly. She peered through the gloom at Taylor. "Let's go into the kitchen. Your mother promised to fix some nice English muffins with jam, and a hot pot of tea, two of my favorite things."

"Oh, yummy," agreed Taylor, who didn't like muffins. "I'll be right there."

Upstairs, she keyed SUNSET. Aunt Cissy was a little chubby. She didn't need English muffins and jam, Taylor decided.

Back in the kitchen, Taylor watched her mother put the teapot on the table and plunk two muffins in the toaster. Then Mrs. Benson turned on the hanging lamp above the kitchen table. "Oh, *no!*" She flipped the light switch several times, not wanting to believe her eyes. What was the matter with this house?

"Anne, your lights are a mess here! That other light down by the sink will *have to do.* Now sit down, and we'll have our muffins and tea. Sit next to me, Taylor. We haven't had our talk yet."

Taylor's mother gulped her tea and prayed for the muffins to pop up. So far her sister-in-law's visit had been a flop.

"Anne? Aren't they about ready?" Aunt Cissy moved the jam pot closer to her plate. "I can just *taste* them."

Mrs. Benson looked down into the toaster. No red coils of heat shone against the muffins. "Why, it's stone cold! The silly thing hasn't even started to toast!" She checked the plug. "I don't understand it. We had toast for breakfast . . . and that light was on then, too."

"Anne, obviously you've got problems. First my room and now this. You'd better call the power company or your builder or somebody! This is ridiculous!" She looked longingly at the jam pot and the package of cold muffins. "How about the broiler?"

"Brilliant! You have good ideas, Cissy." The cheer in Anne Benson's voice was thin, but determined.

Taylor squirmed in her chair. "Let me get my school yearbook to show you. Be right back." Upstairs, she gave a new instruction to 10-X. MEDIAN, she typed.

Five agonizing minutes went by. Then Taylor heard Aunt Cissy's voice. "You mean *that* doesn't work either? Now, Anne, this is absurd! You can't live in a house where nothing works! You should *never* have left the old house. It was utterly charming."

"All of this equipment worked earlier today," asserted Mrs. Benson in tones of steel. "And I left the charming old house because we couldn't afford to keep it up. Is that clear?"

Perched on the top step, Taylor listened to the conversation in the kitchen below her. Her resolve to get rid of Aunt Cissy hardened like a rock within her.

"Anne, I apologize. I guess one of the reasons I came was to look for little pieces of Jim, and of course, I don't find any in this house." Her voice broke.

Taylor heard her mother walk across the kitchen and the scrape of her chair as it was pulled up to the table. Her voice, its anger gone, came up the stairwell. "I know, Cissy. I kept looking for pieces of him too, and it just didn't work. He's gone, and we have to face it. I have to look ahead, not back, and so do you." Mrs. Benson sniffed slightly and cleared her throat.

On the stairs in the dark, Taylor fidgeted. Yes, she and Aunt Cissy had shared a love, along with all the Bensons. Jim Benson had been loved by many. *So why isn't he here?* raged Taylor. *Why do we have to have nosy old Cecilia Benson instead of my father?* The unexplainable injustice of it infuriated Taylor. *Well, Aunt Cissy will pay,* she reminded herself. *I'll make her pay.*

39

"Drink your tea, Cissy," Taylor heard her mother say. "Try not to think about muffins. Tomorrow I'll have the power company out here. Let's go in the living room and watch your program now."

Taylor listened to the teacups clank in the sink and then crossed the floor silently to 10-X.

100%.

THANK YOU. IT WAS NOTHING.

"Oh, but it was," whispered Taylor.

FOWL, she typed, pressing each key firmly.

"Anne, look at that!" came Aunt Cissy's voice from the living room. "The light's on in my room! I'll just run in there and unpack."

Moments later Aunt Cissy's measured steps returned to the living room. In spite of the gift of light, she had not finished her lectures about the new house. The living-room rocker creaked, and Aunt Cissy continued on. "The circuits to this place are totally mixed up. Most ridiculous thing I ever saw."

"Amen to that." Taylor's mother had regained her sense of humor. Both Benson women waited for the television to come on.

"Here's my yearbook, Aunt Cissy." Taylor dropped the book in her aunt's lap and sat down on the sofa. Cissy Benson's eyes never left the TV screen.

"Anne . . ." began Cissy.

"Don't say it! Let me check that socket."

"Anne, it isn't going to work. I am going to miss my program because this house absolutely refuses to cooperate." Aunt Cissy stood up, the yearbook falling to the floor. "I'm tired now anyway, after the drive and all this nonsense with your electricity. It's chilly tonight, and bed will feel good. Anne, I do hope the power company will be here in the morning." She added pointedly, "You know how fond I am of afternoon television."

"When do your programs start?" Mrs. Benson sighed.

"At one o'clock. That gives the power company all morning to sort this out. Good night, dear," said Aunt Cissy, offering her cheek to be kissed. Taylor kissed her aunt's cheek; then Mrs. Benson kissed it. Taylor thought about kissing. Kissing Aunt Cissy meant nothing to her, not now anyway. "See you all in the morning," said Aunt Cissy.

Taylor said good-night to her mother and went upstairs. She waited for the house noises to subside, then keyed 100%.

THANK YOU. IT WAS NOTHING.

Taylor smiled as she got ready for bed. Pretty funny. Nothing had gone right since Aunt Cissy's arrival. Her sister Beth would be proud of her. Yup. Controlling electricity was something. She hadn't realized how much they depended on electricity until the glitch. But now *she* was in control.

Still, control of thought was not so easy. Once again Taylor's mind roamed in the dark and found her father. Restlessly she turned in bed, wishing she could go to sleep just one time without seeing her father's smile, hearing his voice. But for the first time, she was relieved that he was not around. He would not like the way she had treated his sister—not like it at all!

Taylor forced herself to plan ahead for the next day, to dream up more misery the new house could inflict on Aunt Cissy.

Her electric blanket, she thought. Aunt Cissy herself had said what a cool night it was. Taylor shot across the room to 10-X.

BEBOP.

HALLELUJAH! GIVE ME A JOB.

DAYLIGHT.

Taylor went back to bed. No sense in making Aunt Cissy comfortable. If she froze all night, she'd go home tomorrow.

41

"Thank you very much. The address is Number Four King's Court, and please come quickly. We'll be watching for the truck." Taylor's 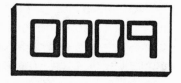 mother hung up the phone and began fixing breakfast.

"Cissy," she greeted her sister-in-law, "the power company absolutely promised to be here before noon. And good morning!" Mrs. Benson grinned, obviously trying to start her guest's day off on a cheerful note.

"Well, they'd better be. Anne, I don't see how you stand it. I froze all night, there's *no light* in my room again, and the TV refuses to work. It's *inexcusable.*" Cissy's lips clamped together.

Mrs. Benson closed her eyes briefly, then began breaking eggs into a bowl. She said nothing. Taylor thought that the eggs were being rapped against the counter *very* firmly.

Okay, Taylor said to herself, *time you got out of town, Aunt Cissy.* On her way to the cupboard for juice glasses, she patted her mother on the shoulder. *I'm really trying to help, Mother. Just give me a little time.*

All that morning the electric circuits at the Benson house worked perfectly. Taylor wanted to be sure that the power company saw 4 King's Court in correct working order. While she waited for the truck to come and find nothing wrong, Taylor began unpacking the boxes in her room. It was time her books were on the shelves where they belonged.

Having so many books of my own is wonderful, Taylor said to herself as she unpacked. Unpacking them was hard, though. Many had been gifts from her father. Inside *The Story of Ferdinand* he had written: "To Taylor, who knows how to be herself. Hugs and Kisses, Daddy." She had called him Daddy when she was little. Being little had been simple.

And the big, colorful books on birds. She opened the

cover of the first volume of her set. There her father had said: "For my student on her twelfth birthday. If you don't watch out, you're going to be the smartest person in this family. With love and pride, Father." She'd first read that on May Day, four short months ago, the last birthday of hers that her father would ever see.

At first, the inscriptions were so painful that they were all Taylor could think of. Gradually, as she held the bird books, her curiosity about geese surfaced. She would have a bird of her own pretty soon, and she knew nothing about young geese. She turned the pages and found a full section on geese, with special notes on snow geese. Taylor read that a blue goose like Chloe was really a snow goose in "the blue phase." Her scientific name was *Chen caerulescens.*

The more she read, the more she questioned her decision to adopt Chloe Minerva. Baby geese took constant care. They called for their mother three or four times an hour all day long, and they kept right on calling until they got an answer. One naturalist recommended carrying the gosling around in a little basket, so that it could see and hear its "mother" all the time. Taylor wasn't sure she wanted to cart a basket everywhere she went for several weeks.

I really don't want to do that! Taylor said to the invisible naturalist in her book. *But I don't want a neurotic goose either.* She rolled over on her back and stared at the peaked roof, thinking. How could she keep Chloe warm and reassured without being with her every blasted minute?

"This Number Four King's Court?" asked a voice downstairs.

"It is. Come right in. My name is Anne Benson, and this house is electrically sick!" Taylor listened to her mother's brief speech and decided to go downstairs.

Taylor perched on the edge of the rocker and listened

while her mother recited the problems with the new house. The repairman listened also, except that every now and then he grinned. The more he grinned, the madder Anne Benson got.

"I can see you think I'm making this all up!" She put her hands on her hips and fixed the repairman with a stern look.

"No ma'am, no sir, not a bit. I mean, we get calls like this all the time. Well, not exactly *all* the time, but we've had our share." Again he grinned.

"See here, young man," interrupted Aunt Cissy. "This is no laughing matter. My programs are due to come on that television set"—she pointed a finger and shook it—"in exactly forty-five minutes. It hasn't been working, and that is the fault of *your company!*" Aunt Cissy's silvery curls bounced as she spoke, and her dark eyes snapped. Occasionally her false teeth jarred against each other because she was talking too fast.

Taylor decided she'd better go back upstairs before she burst out laughing and gave herself away. Silently she slipped out of the room and up the steps.

Upstairs, Taylor thought she'd better make very sure that all the circuits were working correctly. She gave 10-X the instructions and then relaxed, leaning forward, propping her elbows on the computer. The warmth of the machine felt good, since the unusual late August cold snap had lingered. She looked out her window and watched wind whip the branches of the trees, sending leaves to the ground way before their time. Soon fall would come, and school, and then all the leaves would be gone. The earth would turn cold around her father. Too bad he couldn't have taken 10-X with him for warmth. 10-X generated a lot of heat.

Heat! Sure, that's a great idea! Taylor stepped back and examined her computer anew. It had a broad top which was always warm when the machine was running. *If I set*

44

a cage up here, Chloe would be warm as toast. She thought harder. Maybe . . . maybe the computer could even answer Chloe when she peeped for a mother signal. If 10-X could be programmed to reply, then Chloe would be reassured.

Wasn't there a box somewhere with the music board in it, the treat her father had ordered before he died? Was it only last spring they had planned for 10-X to play the music of Beethoven, Bach, even Scott Joplin? *Where was that box?*

"Well? Now what?" Voices from downstairs interrupted Taylor's thoughts. She tiptoed to the top of the steps, then went downstairs to see for herself what was going on.

"Ma'am, everything works. I tested each circuit, and you ran the appliances yourself. All the fuses are okay. It all works." The repairman shrugged his shoulders and headed for the door. "Hope you enjoy your program, ma'am," he said to Aunt Cissy.

"How do we know it won't happen again?" Mrs. Benson opened the door but stood in the way so that the repairman couldn't escape.

"Geez, ma'am, I don't know. All I know is it's working fine now. Maybe you had some unusual power surges. But it's *all okay now.* You saw for yourself." He edged toward the door.

"Very well." Taylor's mother sighed, moving away from the door. "But if there are problems, you people can expect another call. And the next time I want to see your supervisor."

"Sure thing, ma'am. Good-bye now." He hustled out the door and down the sidewalk, disappearing into his truck. Once inside, with the door closed, he radioed his supervisor at the power company.

"This is Eagle Claw, calling Sitting Bull. Hey there, chief? This house on King's Court? Number Four? Yeah, well, the whole crew's nutsy. I wouldn't send no more

45

trucks here if I was you. There's no trouble here. Got that? Ten-four." The truck and its repairman drove away.

As silently as she had come, Taylor faded back up the steps. She crossed the floor to 10-X.

BEBOP.

HALLELUJAH! GIVE ME A JOB.

FOWL, keyed Taylor. Now she could check the computer manual in peace. 10-X was going to be programmed to be Chloe's mother. She would find the music board. Instead of a Beethoven concert for her mother, the music board would *be* a mother. She was sure she could find it, and she could start by going through the boxes in the basement.

Taylor was in the basement, going through the un-packed moving boxes, when she heard Aunt Cissy's voice raised in anger.

"Anne, this is inexcusable! It worked only a few minutes ago, and now it refuses! Isn't there someplace we could go, some friend in the neighborhood, whose house operates properly?"

Taylor heard her mother's voice, low and patient. She couldn't hear the words, but she could guess. *How can she go on being so nice?* Taylor stormed silently. *Well, not me!* She shoved a pile of boxes into a corner. Where was that music board? It *had* to be here; boxes didn't sprout wings and fly away.

"Taylor?"

"In the basement, Mother."

Mrs. Benson came to the basement steps to talk. "We're going down to Stout's for a while so Aunt Cissy can watch her programs. Want to come along?"

"Thanks, but I'm trying to get ready for Chloe." Taylor lowered her voice. "When's she going home?" she hissed.

Her mother shook her head and shrugged her shoulders. "Not yet. Don't worry about it, Taylor. I can handle it."

46

The Benson women left the house, Aunt Cissy urging haste in a loud voice. Taylor turned to another pile of boxes and was rewarded at last. There it was, a large cardboard container marked with blue writing. "PERIPH-ERALS UNLIMITED," it said. Inside was the music board that would reproduce musical sounds, and goose sounds were musical. Sort of. That's what her book had said.

Taylor trudged upstairs, lugging the heavy box. The music board had arrived after her father's death and had never been opened. Opening it now, making it work, studying its possibilities—all that the music board repre-sented was painful. Taylor put the box on the bed and looked at it, her face a set mask. Her chin rose and she spoke to 10-X as though it were a person. "No Beethoven yet. First, a little 'Mother Goose.' Ha-ha-ha." But the attempt to joke made her feel better, and she settled on her bed to read the installation booklet that had been packed with the music board. She read until she was sure she understood each step. She found an old magazine with an article on music boards as peripheral equipment. She read most of the afternoon. Then she called Stacy.

"Chloe will be ready when you are," Stacy said. "Just let me know, and I'll bring her over. Why don't you come here now? Your mom and Aunt Cissy are here, and I'm bored."

Taylor heard the lonesomeness in Stacy's voice. She was sure Stacy was bored. She'd be bored, too, without 10-X, but she had things to do, and Stacy would have to manage for herself. "Thanks, Stacy, but I'm working with 10-X today. See you tomorrow, though, if you can come over with Chloe. I think I'll be ready by then."

Taylor spent the next hour preparing 10-X for mother-hood. It was late afternoon when she heard her mother and aunt come in the door. "Taylor?" Cecilia Benson called from the foot of the stairs. "Bring me your curling

47

iron. I want to do my hair before dinner."

Taylor's brows frowned darkly. Do her hair? Why couldn't she go *home* to do her hair? "Sure, Aunt Cissy. I'll bring it right down." She took the curling iron downstairs and went right back upstairs. She was thinking about Beth and the bright yellow paint, about the vacuum cleaner and the code word "super." *It's time Aunt Cissy got the message,* Taylor muttered to herself, *time one of us girls stood up and fought back. I said she'd pay, and she's going to pay—now. Beth was right when she said, "Stick to your guns."* 10-X was a super gun!

Taylor stood ready, examining her "gun." She waited until she heard the shower in the downstairs bathroom.

BEBOP.

HALLELUJAH! GIVE ME A JOB.

Taylor listened to the downstairs noises. She heard the shower turn off. Then the bathroom door opened, and footsteps went into the guest room. The door to that room shut. She imagined a towel rubbing short hair until it was nearly dry. Then she visualized the curling iron being plugged into the outlet on the east wall, the outlet next to the dresser. The curling iron would set two rows of rigid silver pipes across Aunt Cissy's forehead.

SUPER. Taylor closed her eyes and listened.

"Oh, *my God!* Ooh, oooh, oh, no!" Aunt Cissy's cry subsided into low moans.

"Cissy! Cissy!" Taylor heard her mother call as she ran into the downstairs hall. "What's the matter?" Several short knocks sounded on Cissy's door. "I'm coming in!" warned Mrs. Benson.

Taylor swallowed nervously. Perhaps more had happened than she had anticipated. Maybe she'd better go downstairs and say something helpful. Slowly and quietly she went down the steps.

In Aunt Cissy's room Mrs. Benson stood still, her nose twitching. "What's that awful . . . ?" she sniffed.

Aunt Cissy turned to face Taylor, who was now peering around the doorframe, and Taylor's mother. One of the aunt's hands held the hotly smoking curling iron. The other hand held the remains of a long silver curl. Across her forehead was an inch of singed hair, looking much like the start of a butch haircut. It, too, was smoking.

The sight of Aunt Cissy's stricken face was too much

for Taylor. She could say nothing helpful.

"Oh, Cissy. Oh, *Cissy!*" cried Taylor's mother. "How did it happen? Didn't you test the iron first to see how hot it was?"

Cissy nodded. She put the curling iron in its metal rest and sat down on the bed. Wordlessly she stared at the little pile of hair in her hand.

"I'll get you a scarf, Aunt Cissy," Taylor said in a small voice. She turned and ran upstairs. The result of her "gun" had been more spectacular than she expected, but the thing was done. Maybe *now* Aunt Cissy would go home. Taylor gave 10-X the instructions to return to normal, but she didn't feel as good about it as she had thought she would.

Dinner that night was a solemn affair. Aunt Cissy wore Taylor's scarf over her hair, but the singed area was visible anyway. It looked dreadful. Just as Taylor was about to tell her aunt how fast her hair would grow out, Aunt Cissy began talking about the Stouts. She told Taylor that her friend Stacy was as fat as a butterball. Taylor didn't argue back, though she wanted to. Nor did she tell Aunt Cissy that her hair would grow back. Aunt Cissy was impossible!

That evening Taylor's mother gave Aunt Cissy a home permanent to help hide the damage done by the curling iron. Taylor had to read magazine stories aloud to keep Aunt Cissy happy during the permanent. The entire time she read she got madder. Her aunt had not said one word about going home. Not one measly word. Something more drastic would have to be done.

Now what? Taylor asked herself that night in the dark of her bedroom. She listened as the house became quiet and the women downstairs settled themselves for sleep. She heard an uneven snore from Aunt Cissy's room. *Snoring means too comfortable,* she decided. She tiptoed to the top of the stairs. Then down the stairs and into the kitchen. Silence.

One by one, Taylor turned on the lights in the living room and the hall and kitchen. Then she crept upstairs, an idea taking shape in her mind.

BEBOP.

HALLELUJAH! GIVE ME A JOB.

BOMB, keyed Taylor. Off went all the downstairs circuits. She sneaked back down the steps and turned on the TV, setting its volume at high. She turned on the radio in the kitchen and tiptoed back upstairs. The house was completely quiet. Not even a clock could tick. Taylor waited about five minutes.

100%.

Lights blazed. The hall clock bonged two o'clock. The refrigerator motor ground into action.

"You dirty rat!" James Cagney rasped from the living room. The radio screeched a late-night interview across the empty kitchen.

Upstairs, under her covers, Taylor giggled. With a smile, she listened, waiting for Aunt Cissy to denounce the new house one more time.

"Anne? ANNE?" Aunt Cissy shrilled. Taylor could hear a glass tumble to the floor. "Dammit!" cursed Aunt Cissy, who *never* swore. Taylor almost laughed out loud. The glass holding Aunt Cissy's teeth must have fallen to the floor.

"Coming, Cissy, coming!" Mrs. Benson's voice filled the house with reassurance. "Just let me turn off some of these lights and noises." Taylor heard her mother's swift progress through the downstairs.

"Well, the man from the power company was right. Everything works." Mrs. Benson sounded amazingly cheerful for two in the morning.

"Anne? I want you to *leave this house! Immediately!*" Taylor stifled another laugh. Aunt Cissy was mad all right. Her voice was so piercing the Stouts could probably hear her a block down the street.

Taylor heard her mother's firm speech in reply. "Cissy, I don't wish to be rude to you, but that is not your decision. This electricity problem will be sorted out, I assure you, but *this* is where we live now, and I do not intend to leave. So you'd better settle down, get some sleep, and quit worrying about us. Good night."

Hmmph, thought Taylor. It certainly didn't sound as if her mother were ready to give up on the new house. Aunt Cissy didn't like it, though. *Oops,* she thought. She got out of bed, tiptoed to 10-X, and complimented it for doing a fine job. Then she keyed F OWL in case she overslept in the morning and Aunt Cissy thought she wanted to watch television. She patted 10-X and thought what fun it would be to tell Beth all about Aunt Cissy's visit. Of course, it wasn't so nice for Mother. But it would soon be over, and they both could wave Aunt Cissy good-bye.

In the morning, Mrs. Benson phoned the builder and had a long discussion about electricity and fuses and main transformers. The builder promised to bring his electrician and inspect 4 King's Court that very morning.

Taylor woke up to hear her mother retelling the story of their house. When she heard a man curse and stomp down to the basement, she hopped across the floor to 10-X.

"Mrs. Benson!" the builder hollered from the basement. "I found a problem down here. The circuit on the south wall is dead."

BEBOP.

HALLELUJAH! GIVE ME A JOB.

100%. Taylor let out her breath.

THANK YOU. IT WAS NOTHING.

Taylor leaned against 10-X, blinking her eyes and trying to wake up. She heard her mother's steps cross the kitchen toward the basement stairway. "Are you absolutely positive?" called Mrs. Benson. "My washer and dryer are to be installed there any day now. And I think that the television up here is on that circuit."

"Oh, I'm sure all right," said the builder.

"Now, Mother," inserted Taylor, who had thrown on her bathrobe, grabbed her radio and raced downstairs, "don't get upset. I'll just test it with my radio. If the radio works, it's okay."

Mrs. Benson gave her a strange look. *"Test it with your radio?"* She stared intently at Taylor. "When did you become so interested in electricity?"

"Well, uh, it's important. I mean, we've had so much trouble here, and everything. And . . . and, besides, if there's all this mixup, I can't work 10-X, right?" Taylor ran downstairs before her mother thought up any more questions.

Mrs. Benson sat down on the top step and leaned her head against the wall.

"I'll be *dam* . . . er, *darned!*" said the builder to Taylor. "How'd you come to trot that radio down here?" His chin jutted forward. "Our equipment got no response from this outlet not three minutes ago."

"Just unlucky, I guess. Maybe you should check it again with your equipment. Seems to work fine now. Can I turn off my radio?"

"Sure! Sam, get your stuff back over here and see what's the matter with this outlet! This wiring system shouldn't give *anybody* problems!"

Taylor walked quickly back upstairs, past her mother, and on up to her room. She turned 10-X off, not wanting its hum to attract attention. Phew! That had been squeaky. She could still hear the two men's voices raised in anger way below her in the basement. Maybe, she decided, it would be smart to stay downstairs now for a while. She had planned to ask the builder about his wiring but *now* did not feel very comfortable. Everyone was too edgy.

"Anne, I'm glad you got the builder into this," Aunt Cissy was saying as she pushed a large pin through her hat into the newly curled silver. "I'm leaving you two before I planned to, but I need my *sleep*. Taylor, I'm really sorry to go, but Aunt Cissy is an old lady and not in the mood for electrical wars. You be good now and help your mother. And remember what I said about those fingernails.

"I'll be checking on you by phone, Anne, but I'm not coming back until this house behaves itself."

Cecilia Benson turned and marched out the door. "If I drive a little faster than usual," she tossed over her shoulder, "I'll be home in time for my afternoon programs."

"Did the builder say any-
thing special, Mother?" Taylor gazed out the window
and tried to sound as casual
as possible.

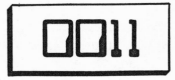

"I think he's confused, but he didn't want me to know
that, of course. He said something about power surges and
this new wiring system, but he didn't make himself clear.
He and his electrician were having an argument about it,
too, which doesn't make me feel very comfortable, but
everything tests normal now. For whatever that's worth!"

"Then we can relax."

"I'm going to read the help wanted ads and try to forget
about it. What are you going to do today?" Mrs. Benson fixed Taylor with a pair of eyes that could not be ig-
nored.

"Get ready for Chloe. Stacy's bringing her pretty soon.
You want to know what I've been working on up there all
this time?"

"I certainly do," replied Mrs. Benson a shade grimly.

Taylor knew that her mother only seemed vague about
computers. Just because she used to teach English litera-
ture didn't mean that she was a dodo on other subjects.
Therefore, Taylor gave a detailed recital on baby geese,
their need for constant reassurance, their growing patterns, everything. She explained how the music board
would let 10-X be Chloe's mother.

"Are you sure you want the goose if it's all that trouble?"

"Oh, yes! Very much." Taylor stopped. She did want
Chloe, but even she wasn't sure why.

"At any rate," Mrs. Benson enunciated precisely, "I
would rather have you taking care of Chloe than working
with that computer all the time. It isn't healthy to hide
yourself away up there all alone."

Taylor listened. In her own way, her mother was serving notice. No doubt about it, she was suspicious of the electrical problems at 4 King's Court. Quickly Taylor spoke. "I guess, except that there really isn't anything to *do* here. Or anybody that I really *know*. And 10-X does have to be Chloe's mother, or else I have to cart her around all the time. Anyhow, couldn't I have a guest now? Now that Aunt Cissy's gone home?"

"Fine. I said that the girls could come, and I meant it. Whom did you have in mind?"

"How about Karen? Could she come for dinner and the night, after I get Chloe settled? Soon, I mean?"

"That'd be nice. A weekend night might be easier for her parents. Why don't you call and arrange it while I read the want ads? Maybe I can get another teaching job, or something new and different. Like editing or working for a newspaper. Who knows?" She smiled with determination and began hunting through the daily paper.

Taylor went directly to the telephone. She knew Karen's number by heart. Dialing that number made her feel better than anything had for days.

"Taylor? Where are you?"

"Up here. With the old guinea pig cage. It's sure lucky we moved it and didn't throw it out."

Downstairs, Mrs. Benson smiled. "Is that for Chloe?"

"Yup. Stacy's bringing her over in an hour or so. Are you ready to leave for that interview?"

"That's what I wanted to tell you. I don't know when I'll be back, but I wrote the number of that company on the phone pad in case you have to reach me. See you later."

There was a brief silence, and then Taylor heard a voice, very low, from the hall below her. "Good luck to you, Anne Benson," the voice said sadly. Then Taylor knew that her mother was afraid. It wouldn't be a lark after all, hunting for a job.

My mother, Taylor said to herself as she worked with Chloe's cage, *is a very good actress.* She reached for the last of the grass she had gathered and patted it into place on the bottom of the cage. Grass had to be pulled from a meadow three blocks away. Maybe she wouldn't have to do it very often. "Dummy," she said out loud. "You'll probably have to get fresh grass every day. It'd be nothing if we had our old backyard full of our own grass. Stupid new house anyway!"

Taylor sat down at the computer console and checked her program again, just to be sure. Yes, the audio system worked. She had tested it by a miniprogram with few instructions. Whenever she said, "Boo!" into the microphone, the music board replied with a set of three tones. It sounded like "Aah, ooh, eee," in a singsong she translated as "Hall-ow-een." It wasn't Scott Joplin and certainly not Beethoven, but it was musical, and it worked.

The new program was instructed to reply only to the call of the gosling, a sort of "peep, peep, peep?" that ended on a questioning note. Then the music board answered with low, soothing tones meaning "I am a mother goose." It sounded like "Zung, ung, ung."

"This'd better work," Taylor said to all of her equipment. She wanted Chloe to come, but she didn't want her to be ever-present. She didn't want anything hanging on her, demanding attention. She didn't know what she wanted anymore. It was an unpleasant feeling. Nothing was right, and everything was wrong. And she was stuck not knowing what to do. If only everything could be like it was before. There. That's what she wanted. "Hah!" she said sadly.

"Hey! It's me. You up there?"

Taylor leaned forward to look out the dormer window. "Hi, Stacy. Did you bring Chloe?"

"Sure. Can we come up?" Stacy's round face was cheerful and sunburned. Part of Taylor's black spirit stirred and began to drift away.

"I think you're going to be lucky," Stacy said as she walked across the bedroom rug toward Taylor and 10-X. "Chloe didn't even look back when I took her away from the others. And Sally and Honker were so busy munching grass that they didn't see me take her. Honker's too dumb to count babies anyway." She giggled.

"Here's the cage. How'd she get so big?" Taylor frowned as the gosling was slipped into the guinea pig cage.

"It's been several days since you saw her, and geese grow fast. She'd be ready to eat by Thanksgiving."

"How can you say that? It sounds so cruel. I'll never understand how people can eat animals they've raised."

"All farmers do. Animals are livestock. House pets are different. I'd never eat a cat or a dog. But we all eat beef and pork and chicken. Maybe a ham was somebody's pet once. Look at Wilbur in *Charlotte's Web*. He almost got eaten."

"Yeah." Taylor smiled. "I loved that book. Mother gave it to me when I was eight, and I read it three times before I'd read anything else."

"You have more books than anybody I've ever known. Could I borrow one sometime?"

"Okay by me. That's what books are for, my father always said—to share. He gave me lots of the books over there." Taylor pointed toward the shelves that stood on either side of her bed.

"Peep, peep, peep?" Chloe uttered plaintively from her cage.

ZUNG, UNG, UNG, hummed the computer's new equipment.

Chloe cocked her head in the direction of the microphone. "Peeep, peeeep?"

58

ZUNG, UNG, UNG. Taylor and Stacy looked at one another and barely breathed.

"Keep talking," urged Stacy. "Chloe's used to human voices. Maybe we can fool her while she figures out she's all right here. She's the calmest one of the batch, so maybe it'll be okay."

"What if it isn't okay? My bird book said she'd have to feel there was a mother near or she'd peep herself to death."

Stacy shrugged her shoulders. "You could always *wear* her in a backpack." Stacy's eyes danced.

"That'll be the day!"

"Peep, peep, peep?"

ZUNG, UNG, UNG. Again, Chloe peered at the equipment with one bright eye.

"Maybe we could take her outside for a while, let her follow us around," suggested Stacy.

Taylor lifted the weighted door of the cage, and Chloe hopped into her hand as if she'd been doing it every day of her life. Carefully Taylor held the gosling as they went downstairs and out to the backyard. Chloe was very soft, very warm, and, Taylor sighed, very dependent.

"Hey, isn't that grass?" Taylor bent down to look at the dirt beside the garage.

"That's what we call it at our place."

"Come on. You know what I mean. Isn't that new grass growing?" Taylor's nose was practically touching the ground.

"Sure it's grass! What'd you expect? Your mom sowed grass seed right after you moved in. She said you hated the mud, and she wasn't too wild about it herself. Didn't you think it would grow?"

"I didn't even know it had been planted." Taylor straightened up, still holding Chloe in her hands.

"Peep, peep, peep?"

"Now what?" Taylor opened her hands and looked hesitantly at the gosling.

"You answer, that's what. Say 'Zung, ung, ung' just like the computer did. It sounded pretty good. I was surprised."

"Peep, peep, peeeeep?" Chloe's call was louder, a bit shrill.

"Zung, ung, ung," answered Taylor. "I feel like a dope."

"You'll get used to it," teased Stacy.

"Feeling like a dope? Super." Taylor shook her head and put Chloe down on the ground near her feet.

"That's better. Do you know that's the first joke you've made since I met you? You have a nice smile, too. You're pretty anyway. There's going to be a line of boys a mile long outside your house after one day in school."

Taylor was shocked. She didn't know any kids who talked like Stacy. Girls didn't tell other girls how pretty one of them was. And what right did Stacy have telling her she never joked? "I'm sorry," she said stiffly.

"No, it's me," mumbled Stacy, her cheerfulness gone. "I'm too honest. I say whatever I'm thinking. I didn't mean to hurt your feelings, especially when your father just died and all. But it's the *truth*," she added defiantly. Her round chin lifted, and she looked Taylor in the eye. "You *are* pretty! I always notice when someone is pretty because I wish *I* were!"

"But you are!" Taylor was surprised Stacy didn't know. "You really are. And when you lose weight, like you said you were going to, you'll be really something." She stopped, embarrassed.

"It's not necessary to try to make me feel better," Stacy said formally. She moved away, following Chloe toward the back of the yard, where tall trees shaded a wide area.

"Hey, look! You said you were too honest, so I was honest with you. I meant it! I wouldn't lie to you." Taylor followed the retreating Stacy and the gosling through the tender blades of young grass.

Stacy threw herself down on the ground under the trees. Chloe peeped gently and hopped up on Stacy's stomach. Stacy put her hands behind her head, leaning against the trunk of an old maple. She let out a big, sad sigh. "Thanks. I must just be grumpy today. Mama said I was this morning. But I'm so bored I could die! And I'm not losing weight—I'm gaining it. Since that night you and your mom were over at our place I've gained a whole pound. Sixteen ounces!" Stacy looked as if she would cry any second.

"Gee, that's too bad." Taylor was genuinely sorry that Stacy had gained weight. "How do you suppose that happened?"

Stacy sat up and stared at the back of the Bensons' house. "I *thought* I was on a diet. Mama said I've been eating without realizing it. Just because I was bored. There's nothing to *do* here! On the farm I had a horse and chickens and baby animals all over the place. I don't have a computer to hide away with like you do."

"Did my mother say that? That I was hiding away with 10-X?"

Stacy turned to look at Taylor. "Yes, but she didn't have to. I could see it. But that's okay with me, if it helps. I understand."

Again Taylor was jolted by Stacy's words. She was terribly honest. That openness robbed Taylor of words, and for some time she couldn't think of anything to say.

"I suppose," she began slowly, "that if you're hiding, you don't know when somebody sows grass seed, do you?"

Stacy nodded. Taylor looked down between her knees at the new grass. What else had her mother done that she didn't know?

With kindness, Stacy put her hand on Taylor's shoulder. "Don't worry about it. Your mom just wants you to

61

be happy here, that's all, like my folks want me to be happy. It'll probably get better when school starts and we meet more kids and have something to do. *Amō, amās, amat,"* Stacy chanted softly. *"Gallia est omnis dīvīsa in partēs trēs.* . . . I read ahead for next year. That's how Caesar's *Gallic Wars* starts for second-year Latin."

"Of course." Taylor nodded solemnly.

Stacy giggled. "I warned you! Latin's my favorite subject."

"Isn't it hard? I always heard it was hard."

"Nope. Especially not for somebody who likes math. It's regular, sort of, dependable. It has rules, and they work. I just like it, that's all. I love languages. I think I'll be a language major in college."

"You'd like computer talk then. Like the word 'byte.' A byte is a piece of information eight bits long. And a 'nybble' is half a byte."

"I love it." Stacy grinned. "Are you going to major in computers?"

"In computer science. Languages are okay, but computers are more fun." Inspired, Taylor jumped up. "That's what we can do right now! I have some menus in 10-X's memory. Do you want to see them and start your diet?"

"Will it really work? I'm sick of looking like a blob. None of my clothes look like they do in the store on those models. But I get so *hungry.* " Stacy looked defeated by the mere idea of a diet.

"My sister Whitney," assured Taylor as they scooped up Chloe and started toward the house, "said that you only get hungry at first. She had to lose about five pounds when she was a senior, so we've got all her calorie charts."

"Five pounds is nothing," snorted Stacy. "My *nose* weighs five pounds!"

Taylor laughed. "She also said you had to keep busy every minute so you didn't think about food."

"Why did you think about it? To make the diets, I mean."

Briefly Taylor debated about telling Stacy of her code to run the house. No, Stacy'd probably think she was weird. Maybe she *was* weird. After all, would anyone understand the feelings that made her want to mess up life in the new house?

"Peep, peep, peeeep?"

Stacy whispered, "Try to sound as much like 10-X as possible."

"Zung, ung, ung," droned Taylor, feeling foolish again.

"Not bad. It's easy being a goose." Stacy jumped up the steps to Taylor's room two at a time.

Chloe was deposited in the grasses of her cage, and the door slid into place. She poked the cup of mash with her beak and began to eat.

"Where can I get Chloe more food like that?"

"That comes from a big bag I put in your garage. Daddy gets it wholesale from an old friend. He said not to worry about it because we'd always have it. Now. About my starvation."

"You won't starve. Each day you get a thousand calories. Whitney said it's plenty if you don't think about it all the time."

"Ho, ho," said Stacy glumly.

"I have to get those menus out of memory," Taylor mumbled to herself. "Where did I put all that stuff? I wish I had more floppy disks!"

" 'Floppy disks'?"

"Mmhmm," Taylor answered absently. "They're like a forty-five record. They're extra storage space, and they cost money, which I don't have right now."

"You're right, Taylor. Computer language is cool. How does all this equipment work? How do you know how it works?"

"Well, it always works the same, like you said about Latin. I key the information into 10-X, and it's stored in a thing called a memory. Floppy disks are just more memory, okay? I use a program language that my father and I created, plus a compiler program that we wrote. The compiler program is a translator program that tells 10-X what I want it to do. 10-X takes what I type and turns it into machine language to work on it. If I type the wrong stuff, then garbage comes out on the screen."

"That's what diets are, garbage."

"We've got to work on your attitude." Taylor sighed in mock seriousness. "10-X will fix yummy meals for you, just wait."

"But how?"

"It's logic. You have to give each step, or direction, in the right order and not leave out any steps. That's it, mainly."

Taylor keyed B E B O P on the keyboard, slowly, so that Stacy could watch.

HALLELUJAH! GIVE ME A JOB.

Stacy laughed. "It's like a person is hiding in there! Tell him to write me a menu that says I can have cherry pie for lunch and supper."

Taylor typed, BK + LN + 3.1416 + DN + 3.1416 = 1,000.

NO 3.1416.

"Hey! What's that?"

"That's a menu of a thousand calories a day with breakfast normal; that's the BK. For lunch it had to include cherry pie; that's the three point one four one six, and more pie for dinner. When it did that, the menu went over a thousand calories. So the food that messed up the menu was kicked out. Looks like 10-X won't write menus with pie in them."

"*No pie?* But I love desserts! They're my favorite part

of the meal. I can't diet if I can't ever have dessert!"

"There're lots of desserts in the information I gave 10-X, but it doesn't seem to work with cherry pie." Taylor thumbed through a small red calorie book. "Uh-oh. Cherry pie has almost three hundred and fifty calories! That's the most I told 10-X to fix for your *whole lunch*. No wonder it tossed out the pie."

"Then turn him off! If I can't have any of Mama's pies, I won't diet." Stacy stared out the window and blinked rapidly. Her first birthday was recorded on film in the Stouts' library of home movies. She had had not a cake, but a lemon meringue pie with a yellow candle. In the movie her face was covered with lemon and fluffy meringue and a beatific smile. Pie was essential to life.

"Stacy?" Taylor's voice was gentle. "You like pie more than you want to be thin?"

Stacy looked down at her lap and didn't answer.

"It won't take too long to lose weight, and there really are some desserts. After you're thin, you can have pie again once in a while. Your mama said she'd fix the foods 10-X planned, didn't she?"

Stacy nodded.

"Maybe she'd like to lose a few pounds, and your father, too."

"His doctor said he'd have to. For his heart," admitted Stacy.

"Wouldn't that help him live longer if you went on a diet? That way you'd all lose weight. I'd have done it for my father if it would've helped. We didn't even know his heart was bad."

Silently Stacy plucked at the seam of her jeans. She stared at her knees and then at the floor, where the sun made patterns on the celery-colored rug. "All right. I'll do it." She raised her head. "I didn't mean to make you think of your father again. I keep doing that. It makes me feel awful."

"It's not on purpose. I think about him a lot anyhow. Especially when I work with 10-X. Once it made me feel so awful I wanted to smash 10-X with a hammer. Only I couldn't do it."

Stacy shook her head in sympathy. "Come on. Show me the menus. But could you kinda nag me once in a while? I don't think Mama will nag me about staying on the diet."

Taylor smiled. "Yup. I'll keep telling you how skinny you're getting. How about that?" She turned to the computer console and opened a manila envelope marked "DIET." "Okay. Now these instructions at the top tell 10-X to go into memory for a breakfast that's about two hundred to two hundred twenty-five calories. Then it'll make a lunch of about three hundred calories and a dinner of about five hundred. It's going to add up to around a thousand calories a day, like I said."

"Shoot." Stacy looked expectantly at 10-X's display screen while Taylor keyed in the instructions: BK + LN + DN = 1,000. Faster than Stacy could believe, words appeared on the screen.

```
BREAKFAST:
8   OZ.   TOMATO JUICE
          POACHED EGG
1         SLICE PROTEIN BREAD
1/2 PAT   BUTTER
                         201 CALORIES
LUNCH:
1   CUP   CHICKEN BROTH
          TUNA SALAD (4 T. TUNA)
1   CUP   BROCCOLI
1/2 CUP   APPLESAUCE
          TEA (NO SUGAR)
                         296 CALORIES
```

```
SNACK:
4    OZ.   VEGETABLE JUICE
3          RYE KRISPS
                             86 CALORIES

DINNER:
3    OZ.   BROILED FILET OR T-BONE
           STEAK
1/2 CUP   STEWED TOMATOES
1/2 CUP   COOKED BEETS
1   CUP   CABBAGE SLAW
1/2 T     FRENCH DRESSING
1/2 CUP   JELL-O + 1 T. DIET WHIPPED
          TOPPING
          TEA
                            427 CALORIES

SNACK:
5          LIFESAVERS
1          PIECE TOFFEE
                             50 CALORIES
              TOTAL CALORIES: 1,050
```

"It could be worse," quavered Stacy. "But it's over a thousand calories. Did 10-X make a mistake?"

Taylor shook her head. "Computers don't make mistakes like people. This diet is okay. I told 10-X it could have fifty calories either way. My instructions said that nine fifty and one thousand and one thousand and fifty were all the same thing. It was easier that way, and it'll even out."

A huge sigh, beginning in the region of Stacy's socks, rose and finally escaped through her downturned mouth. "At least they're all foods Daddy likes, so he shouldn't mind too much. I'll probably sneak off to the garage and murder a goose. We have a *new* barbecue grill." She squinted and tried to look mean and desperate.

Taylor began to laugh and couldn't stop. In spite of her

misery, Stacy giggled and joined in the laugh. They laughed until their sides ached.

"I hope it's this funny a week from now when I'm dying of hunger," gasped Stacy. She wiped away tears of laughter and looked at the display screen. "Maybe I'd better start copying menus. If I took some home today, Mama could start in right now. Are some of them going to be better than this one?"

"I hope so," agreed Taylor, " 'cause this one sure isn't much." She reached into a drawer and pulled out a yellow pad of paper. "Here. I'll help you copy so it goes faster."

For some time the girls copied menus. Chloe munched her grasses and pecked at her mash. When she peeped, Taylor answered. The sun slipped down, and the upstairs room grew dim.

"Taylor?" Mrs. Benson called up the stairs.

"Hi! We're up here copying menus for Stacy's diet. How'd it go?"

"Come on down, and I'll tell you all about it," sang Anne Benson. The girls heard brisk steps march into the kitchen, and then, "I wonder if that nice little frozen cake survived the move?"

"Peep, peep, peep?" Chloe waddled toward the door of her cage.

ZUNG, UNG, UNG, 10-X soothed promptly. The gosling stared at the equipment so close to her cage. Again she called for an answer, and back came the reassuring sound, uncannily like her mother, Sally. Chloe didn't know what to make of it, but she wasn't frightened. Thoughtfully she pecked her mash. "Peep, peep?" she asked again. With amazing promptness came the musical answer. Chloe returned to the bowl of poultry mash.

Taylor and Stacy, watching Chloe test the computer, smiled as the young goose pecked at her food. "It works," Taylor said.

"We ought to go downstairs. Your mother sounded pretty excited about her interview if you ask me," Stacy said.

100%, keyed Taylor, nodding agreement.

THANK YOU. IT WAS NOTHING.

"What'd you do that for?"

"It's a reward for 'noble performance,' another joke of my father's." Taylor smiled. It was shaky, but it was a smile. "It tells 10-X to get ready for new instructions, or else it means good-bye if we're finished."

Stacy's brow wrinkled in concern. "I don't think I could do that—work with 10-X all the time and know those words were his. Isn't that hard?"

"Yes." Taylor stood up abruptly. "Come on. Don't forget your menus." She double-checked the music board that would answer Chloe, and together the girls went downstairs.

"Ah, here you are," greeted Mrs. Benson. She handed a piece of cake and a glass of milk to each of the girls. "Let's sit down in the living room, and I'll tell you what happened."

"Eat only half," warned Taylor as they settled together on the living-room couch. She looked pointedly at the piece of cake.

"Half?"

"That's better than none," Taylor said firmly.

"To me!" interrupted Mrs. Benson, raising her glass of milk in the air as for a toast.

"To you," chorused Taylor and Stacy. Just as in the movies.

"Now." Mrs. Benson glowed. "Forget about diets for a minute, and let me tell you what happened. *I have a job!* It's unbelievable, I know, but it's true. It really happened, and I'm still pinching myself!"

"What kind of job?" asked Taylor quickly. Her mother looked wonderful, better than she had in months. Taylor was uneasy, somehow, but she was glad. Of course, she was glad.

"I'm a sort of librarian. The interview was with the Man-Trey Company on the edge of Kingswood. It's been here over two years, they said, before the suburb grew enough to meet their property line."

"I know," said Stacy. "It's that big building out on the highway. The one with all the ducks on that little lake out front. It's *beautiful.* What do they do, though?"

Mrs. Benson smiled. "It is a pretty place, Stacy. The man I'm working for is one of the founders, Will Manfred. That's where the 'Man' in Man-Trey comes from. He and I went to high school together." She leaned against the back of the sofa and drank her milk. "That's why I got the job; he knows me. Of course, we hadn't seen each other in years. He was a student in one of your father's classes, Taylor, when he first started teaching at the university."

Taylor set her mouth in a straight line. Her mother was certainly excited about this Will Manfred person. What did he have that was so special? Why was he alive when her father wasn't? She didn't know him, but already she disliked Will Manfred.

"Anyway, I start in about a week, whenever I'm ready, Will said. He is *such* a nice person. And I'll be in charge of planning enrichment classes for employees, their library of company records and business materials, all sorts of different things. It sounds exciting." The mood of satisfaction surrounded her like a thing that could be touched.

"That's neat, Mrs. Benson. My mama'll miss you, but she said you'd be going to work. What does the Man-Trey Company do?"

"Oh, Stacy, I'm sorry. You asked that before, and I was so wound up I forgot to answer. They manufacture small appliances, like electric toothbrushes and traveling irons. I won't need to know too much about that end of it at first, I hope.

"Well, Taylor, what do you think? You haven't said a word." Mrs. Benson looked over her glass of milk at Taylor.

"It's fine, of course. Whatever you want," Taylor said woodenly. "How many hours a day do you work?"

"That's one of the best parts. I don't start until nine, so we can always have breakfast together, and I'll be home by four-thirty at the latest. It pays a little less that way, but Will thought it would work out. Isn't that great?"

"Sure." Taylor tried to feel happier for her mother, but there was a lump in her throat that hurt. Everybody was so *stinky happy* in this dumb neighborhood. When would it be *her* turn?

Anne Benson sighed. She finished her milk and put the glass on the end table. It was obvious to her that Taylor was miserable, but she wasn't sure why.

"Tell me what you two did this afternoon. Is Chloe all settled?"

"I think so." Stacy nodded. "We haven't heard any wild peeping down here, so she must think the computer's

71

answer is okay. That's lucky. Boy, is that lucky."

"Taylor, did you get in touch with Karen? Is she coming for a visit?"

"Yes, I did," answered Taylor, brightening at the thought. "She's coming Friday afternoon, if that's all right. Her mom said she could stay until Saturday afternoon, okay?"

"That's wonderful."

"Who's Karen?" Stacy looked at Taylor.

"She's my best friend. We were babies together, back in Greensboro. She's a junior high cheerleader in my old school, and her boyfriend was my boyfriend's best friend, too." How far away that all sounded.

"I've never had a boyfriend," confessed Stacy. "Boys aren't interested in fat girls who look like they're in third grade."

"I don't have one now. He was a moron anyway, and he's too short. But you'll have one as soon as you lose that weight, honest."

"Taylor's right, Stacy," said Mrs. Benson, "and you won't ever have to worry about boys who are too short. All of our girls have had to hunt for the tallest male around."

"I suppose. Taylor, do you want the rest of my cake? It keeps *looking* at me, kinda pitiful like."

Taylor and her mother laughed. "No cake has the right to do that, Stacy," said Mrs. Benson. "I'll just pack it off to the kitchen so you can forget about it."

"How about some iced tea?" suggested Taylor. "Then we could crunch the ice cubes. See? I know how to nag, sort of."

"Gee, thanks. I guess if I want to lose weight, I'll have to fall in love with tea and ice cubes. Whee." Her face was so doleful that both Mrs. Benson and Taylor smiled.

"Come on," said Taylor. "I'll fix the tea and tell you about Karen."

Waiting for Karen's visit made Taylor restless. She fiddled with 10-X now and then, but no new words popped up to add to the

code. One morning she went shopping with her mother and chose new curtains with a matching bedspread. They made her room look better, but of course, it wasn't the same. In her old bedroom she had had a real fireplace. Its bricks had been painted white, and its wooden mantelpiece was over a hundred years old. Somebody had carved initials and a heart in one corner of the mantel. "B.T. loves J.D." said the heart. Karen had loved that room. What would she think of the new one?

"Peep, peep, peep?" asked Chloe from her cage.

ZUNG, UNG, UNG, hummed Mother 10-X.

Taylor listened as she lay on her bed and waited for time to pass. Three more hours until Karen would come. Chloe was being awfully good. No trouble at all, really. Whenever Chloe peeped into the microphone, the music board answered—it answered only to "peep-peep." Taylor couldn't ask for more. And Chloe was fun. She liked it best outside but didn't fuss when Taylor put her back in the cage. They had spent one afternoon in the meadow, where Taylor gathered grasses for the bottom of the cage. Chloe had thought the meadow some sort of goose heaven.

Taylor looked at her pet now and, like a fond aunt, saw how quickly the goose was growing. Soon she'd be too big for the cage and would move to the garage. "That's okay," she said to Chloe. "I'm pretty tired of 'Zung, ung, ung,' every hour all night long." Chloe tipped her head to one side and looked in the direction of Taylor's voice.

"Never mind, goosie. I hardly notice it anymore." Taylor sat bolt upright on her bed. True. She rarely heard the sound of the music board at night. But how about Karen?

She liked to stay up late and sleep late in the morning. Early every morning Chloe began to peep-peep with greater frequency and vigor. It was hard to ignore her after seven o'clock. "Oh, no," said Taylor in disgust. Karen loved her cat, but what would she think of this peeping goose?

"Taylor? I think our company's here," called Mrs. Benson.

"Mother"—Taylor worried as she ran down the steps—"what are we going to do about Chloe? She'll keep Karen up all night and won't let her sleep in the morning. She's going to hate it here!"

"It's only for one night, honey, and if you're up late talking, I'm sure Karen won't notice."

"Fat chance! You'd have to be deaf not to hear Chloe in the morning."

The doorbell rang, and Mrs. Benson moved to welcome their guests. Taylor and Karen were old friends; so were Mrs. Benson and Mrs. Miller, Karen's mother. The two women planned to visit over coffee until Mrs. Miller went back to Greensboro.

"Greetings, greetings! Happy new house!" chirruped Mrs. Miller as she held forth a large plant tied with a yellow bow.

"Hey, this is decent," approved Karen as she struggled through the door with her suitcase, favorite pillow, and a package. "I have a present, too. Here."

"Thanks a lot. You didn't have to *bring* me something." Taylor fumbled with the wrapping paper and felt strange. She'd never taken a *present* to somebody just for spending the night. It made her feel very out-of-town. Very far away.

Mrs. Miller and Mrs. Benson drifted back to the kitchen, talking as they went. Taylor helped Karen upstairs with her suitcase and pillow. "Not bad. Pretty cool, in fact. Sorta like a cabin at the lake. This wood's nice."

Karen ran her hand over the wood paneling.

"That's what Stacy said," Taylor answered. She opened her present all the way. It was a box of notepaper with Snoopy, the cartoon dog, lying on top of his doghouse. "Thanks. I hardly ever write letters because I'm so lazy, but it'll be fun on this paper."

"Sure. You can write to me!" Karen grinned. "Who's Stacy?"

"Write to you? But we're not that far away!"

"Well, it took us almost an hour to get here. Of course, that's 'cause Mom got lost twice. Can you believe that? Twice!" Karen giggled. "Who's Stacy?" she asked again.

Taylor was quiet. An hour was a lot of driving. She'd been right then. They might as well have moved to Alaska. "Uh, Stacy? She's a little kid who lives down the street. Well, not exactly a kid. She's our age. She just looks like a kid. She gave me Chloe. That's Chloe." Taylor pointed to the cage atop 10-X. Chloe was looking at the girls, listening to the sound of their voices. Chloe liked to hear voices.

"Chloe? What is it, a duck?" Karen walked over to inspect what was in the cage.

"Peep, peep, peep?"

ZUNG, UNG, UNG, answered Mother 10-X.

"Hey! What's that all about?" Karen stared at the computer.

"First of all"—Taylor smiled—"it's a goose, not a duck. And all that stuff is to keep her happy. Geese call for their mother every few minutes. Anyway, it seems like every few minutes. If they don't get an answer, they panic. So I rigged up 10-X to answer her so she'll shut up. It works, too. You wouldn't *believe* all the things I can make my computer do here. Wait till I tell you about Aunt Cissy's visit!" Her head buzzed with all that she wanted to tell Karen.

"But why? I mean, what's she good for? Can you play

with her like I play with Willy?" Willy was Karen's cat.

"Not exactly. But she loves to go for walks. She follows me around like I'm her mother. And she likes to be petted. I don't know why, but she does. I'm going to dig her a pond out back under the trees."

"Yippee. You must be pretty bored, huh?" Karen turned away from Chloe and flopped down on the bed. "I like this spread, but then I like *all* patchwork. It's neat, and it's new, isn't it? This house sure is different from your old one."

"Of course," Taylor said shortly. Why did she feel she should defend Chloe? And it was dumb to say the house was different. Any idiot could see how different it was, just by looking at the outside.

"You should see Suzanne's new haircut," volunteered Karen. "It's little teeny curls all over her head. She just washes it and lets it dry on its own. I'm thinking of getting mine done that way before school starts. What do you think?"

"I like your hair long and straight, just like it is. You've always worn it that way! You don't want to look like Suzanne, do you?"

"Of course not! I wouldn't look like her just because our hair was the same. She's right, though. It's the new style, and mine isn't." Karen ran her hands through her long reddish hair.

"Is she still going with Bruce?" Taylor was eager to hear about everybody. Later she could tell Karen how 10-X ran the house.

"Nope. He's a wimp. There's a new family about two blocks away. Named Cutter, or Crater, something like that. The father's a professor at the university. Anyway, they have a whole bunch of kids, and one of them's an eighth-grade boy. Suzanne likes him now. She thinks he likes her, but I'm not sure. He walked *me* home from the drugstore Wednesday night. He says he's a good basketball player. Since I'm a cheerleader, I'll find out. He's kinda nice, but I'm not sure he's Suzanne's type."

"Bruce isn't a wimp!"

"Suzanne says anybody in eighth grade who talks about his paper route all the time is a wimp. Speaking of losers," teased Karen, "Tom is going with Alison now. Did you know that?"

Taylor felt an unreasonable pang of jealousy. Even though she and Tom were through, even though it was all over, she thought of him as her property.

"Alison? How could he?" She'd been gone only a few weeks. How could so much have happened in that time? Her mind flashed a cartoon of her friends racing around like an old-time movie. Zap! Into the beauty parlor. Snip, snip. Zap! Meet you at the drugstore. Slurp, slurp. Soda gone. Walk you home, Karen? Gee, I'm a good basketball player. Who's Taylor? Zap! Tom loves Alison. Zap! School starting. You can sit in Taylor's seat. She's not here anymore.

Taylor shook her head to get rid of the jerky, awful moving picture show. What did she care if Tom was going with Alison? Alison was a moron, too. Always talking about her family's vacations. "Have you been to the Caribbean? When we were in London last fall. . . ." What a snob.

"Let's go downstairs," Taylor suggested.

It was better in the kitchen with Mrs. Miller and Taylor's mother. They talked about the plays that were coming to the Little Theater on the university campus. Taylor's family had seen all the plays because it didn't cost very much money and all the Bensons loved plays. Mrs. Miller told funny stories about the dentist's office where she worked part time. The dentist had said to say hello to Mrs. Benson and Taylor. Finally, Mrs. Miller put her napkin in her purse and said she had to be going.

"With this map you drew on my napkin I think I can

find my way home." She laughed. "I felt so foolish trying to find you, Anne. I was so sure I knew where I was going! Well, I have to be off. Karen, be a good guest. Your father or I will be here tomorrow afternoon around four o'clock. All right?" She kissed Karen on the forehead and was gone.

"Well, what do you want to do?" Taylor asked Karen.

"I don't know. What's there to do here?"

Taylor shook her head. "Nothing. Absolutely nothing. We could watch TV."

"Girls, why don't you make us something special for dinner? You've always enjoyed puttering around in the kitchen. Surprise me." Mrs. Benson patted Karen on the shoulder. "It's nice to have you here, Karen. Taylor's missed you a great deal." She smiled and went into the living room in search of her book.

"I've missed you, too, Taylor. I didn't think it was so far away. Taylor," said Karen with inspiration, "let's try pizza again. We almost had it that last time. Remember? We made our own crust?"

Taylor remembered. It had been the night before her father died. How did you forget a thing like that? How could Karen be so thoughtless? Her face darkened with memory.

"Geez, what's the matter? Don't you like pizza anymore?"

"That last time was when my father died. Can't you remember *anything?*" Never had she been so angry with Karen.

"I'm sorry, Taylor. I just didn't think of it." She paused and took a deep breath. "And, Taylor, you can't keep thinking about it either. I'm sorry, *honest.* We *all* are. But you've gotta start thinking about other things. It's been three months now, and you're still like this. This is *me, Karen.* Have I ever lied to you?" Karen clasped and unclasped her hands in her lap. She had sat down at the table during her speech, and now she looked up at Taylor miserably.

Taylor could not look at her old friend. She stared down the length of the kitchen, trying to decide how to answer. Finally, she said, "No, you've never lied to me. I just can't seem to help it. I can't forget. Not anything. All I want is for it to be like it was before. And it can't be. I know that."

Karen stood up. She wanted to hold Taylor in her arms like a sister, but it would be embarrassing. Instead, she leaned toward her. "Come on," she urged softly. "Think about us . . . *now.* Your father wouldn't want you to be sad, would he?"

"No, but I don't think he'd want me to forget him right away either." Taylor's back stiffened. In spite of their forever friendship, what Karen had said was like a wound. It hurt.

"Of course not, but he was happy all the time. He laughed a lot, remember? Always making jokes, and piling the car full of kids to go places? And he always talked to me like I was a real person, you know, an adult, not a kid. Even when I was little, he was like that. Nobody's asking you to forget him."

"Then what do you want?"

"Just that you don't think of him with every little thing, like the pizza. It makes it too hard for you. I don't think that's right." Karen's tone was loving.

Taylor felt the love and thawed, because she had to, because maybe Karen was right. Her shoulders sagged, and she turned. "I didn't mean to make you miserable like me. But what am I supposed to do? I told you I can't forget, and it's the truth. I can't." Her voice broke, but she did not cry.

"Yeah, but I think you've gotta put it all away somewhere and just go on. Go on, that's all. Now what're we gonna make for dinner? I'm hungry."

Taylor thought briefly. "Let's try the pizza again. I haven't had any since that time. It sounds good." It sounded awful, but she would eat it if it killed her. Maybe, if she ate the pizza, the memory would go away. Like riding your bike again after a fall.

The minutes began to pass more pleasantly as the girls diced green peppers, browned hamburger, chopped onions, and waited for the dough to rise. Karen talked constantly, filling Taylor in on every newsworthy tidbit she could think of. The drugstore had put in two more tables, so now all the kids had a place to sit. Also, they'd hired another employee, saying it wasn't a drugstore but a teen canteen. Taylor laughed, but the laugh hurt. There was no drugstore like it in Kingswood, she knew that.

When the pizza came out of the oven at last, she was hungry. It tasted good. Even Mrs. Benson, who said pizza made her burp, ate four slices, praising every bite. "I think we ought to patent this one, girls. It's scrumptious."

After dinner, Taylor took Karen on a walk around the new neighborhood. She had never walked through Kingswood Manor, so it was as new to her as it was to Karen. Its very newness was offensive to them both. No elderly oaks arched over the winding streets. No windswept piles of leaves announced the coming of fall. The entire area was dotted with mounds of black Iowa earth, rich, promising lush lawns in the future. Neither Karen nor Taylor could see the promise, so used were they to older neighborhoods, where carefully landscaped lots bordered one another. The hulks of unfinished houses promised only strangers—someday, maybe. Who could tell? Only two streets, plus Taylor's, had houses that were occupied.

"Come up here," called Karen from the top of a huge pile of earth. "There's another place full of houses off that way," she said, pointing to the west.

Taylor scrambled up the dirt pile to look. Sure enough,

there were many streets and houses. And they were finished. Early-evening lights twinkled from second stories as babies were tucked into bed. "There must be a hundred houses or so, don't you think? I couldn't figure out why they'd build a school way out here, but now I know. I wonder where the school is?"

Karen shrugged her shoulders. "Sure is quiet out here. Kinda spooky. But there're going to be lots of people here someday. Let's go on back now. I brought a couple of new albums we could listen to."

Taylor and her guest spent the evening listening to records. Taylor fed Chloe her evening ration of mash and promised to take her to the meadow soon for fresh grasses. Karen was uninterested in Chloe. She didn't want to pet her or hold her. "She'll *do* something on me. I just know it." Taylor put Chloe back in her cage.

When it was time to get ready for bed, Taylor remembered she hadn't told Karen about how 10-X could run the house. She got out the note pad from under the mattress and explained what the symbols meant and what had happened. "You mean you burned up the vacuum cleaner?" Karen was impressed. "Show me something, *please?* Just one little thing? Oh, I wish I'd been here when you chased Aunt Cissy out. I never said anything, but she *is* an old bat." Karen grinned wickedly.

Taylor nodded. "Well, we could do that trick again with the TV and the radio and lights. That was funny. It just comes on, KA-BOOM-BA, out of nowhere."

Karen nodded, delighted. "Yeah. Sounds like a roll, all right."

"What's 'a roll'?"

"Something terribly funny. That new kid says it all the time. I wish you could meet him, Taylor. You'd like him."

"Well, I can't meet him *now,*" Taylor retorted. "Okay, then, let's do it. We have to wait till Mother is asleep.

Then we creep down and set it up, okay?" Taylor felt guilty at the idea of waking her mother. She tried to reassure herself. Well, she isn't working yet or anything. And it's just a joke after all.

For another hour and a half Taylor and Karen talked and waited for Mrs. Benson to go to sleep. Then Taylor tiptoed over to 10-X, turned off the music board, and keyed in her password.

BEBOP.

HALLELUJAH! GIVE ME A JOB.

"Your father was so funny." Karen chuckled softly. She had crept up behind Taylor at the computer.

Taylor closed her eyes briefly. No. Karen was right, and this time she wasn't going to react. "Sssh, now. I'm going to tell 10-X to turn everything off."

BOMB, she keyed quickly. The house fell silent. Minutes passed as the girls listened in case Mrs. Benson woke up. There was no sound. They went downstairs to turn the kitchen radio to its loudest volume, the TV to a deafening pitch, and all the lights to On.

"Let's wait five minutes," suggested Karen when they were upstairs again. Five minutes passed.

100%, typed Taylor.

". . . don't think that was ever logical," screamed a woman through the radio, "giving women's names to all the hurricanes!"

"My darling," hollered a male TV lover, "tell me I am the only man in your life. Tell me I mean everything to you!"

Lights glared rudely throughout the house as Mrs. Benson stumbled into the hallway, blinking and shaking her head.

Upstairs, Taylor smiled halfheartedly as Karen doubled over with laughter.

THANK YOU. IT WAS NOTHING.

"Karen," hissed Taylor, "stop it. Quick. We've got to

go downstairs and act surprised or my mother's going to be suspicious."

"I c-c-can't." Karen giggled. "You go. Say I'm scared or something. But I can't stop laughing." Her voice dissolved into quiet hysterics.

Taylor frowned. Great. She ran over to the steps, hesitated a minute, and then made a carefully slow descent, rubbing her eyes as she went. "What's wrong?" She yawned as she came around the corner into the living room. "Why are the lights on?"

"*You* tell *me!*" her mother snapped angrily. She pulled the plug on the blaring television and snapped off each light. "I thought this was all settled. Where's Karen?"

"Upstairs. She put her head under her pillow and said for me to find out what was the matter," Taylor said uneasily. Her mother looked exhausted.

"Well, this is the *last straw.* I suppose there's nothing wrong *up*stairs. Am I right?"

"I don't think so," said Taylor, her eyes on one button of her mother's pajamas. "I'm too sleepy to tell. I just heard all this noise, so I came down."

"Uh-hunh. I see. Well, I'll call the power company and the builder in the morning and get them out here at the same time. We're going to get to the bottom of this if it's the last thing I do!" Mrs. Benson gave Taylor a look designed to shrivel and stalked to her bedroom.

"She didn't think it was very funny, did she?" whispered Karen as Taylor climbed into bed.

"No. In fact, she's furious. And I'm pretty sure she's figured it out, too." Taylor dreaded telling her mother the truth, but maybe it was time. Maybe, if she explained it right, her mother would agree that it was funny. It had gotten rid of Aunt Cissy, and that was something. Taylor yawned with tiredness and felt rotten about waking up her mother.

An answering yawn came from Karen, who spoke sleepily. "Hey, Taylor?"

"Pfeep, pfeeep, pfeeeeep?" The call was high-pitched and whiny.

"That's what I was going to tell you," said Karen. "That goose's been having a fit. Did you turn her 'mother' off?"

"Yeah. I'll fix it now."

Taylor crept soundlessly across the floor. "Zung, ung, ung," she said as soothingly as possible. Chloe peered at her with one eye.

"Peep, peeep?" she asked.

"Zung, ung, ung," Taylor answered again, sighing. All of a sudden she felt too tired even to move. Too many nights had been nights without sleep. She fumbled with the keyboard, eager to get in bed again. Chloe would wake her up so early in the morning.

Taylor groped for the switch that would turn on the music board and her left hand brushed the edge of the keyboard.

Q, typed itself by mistake.

OOPS! THINK AGAIN, DODO, flashed on the video screen. Taylor stared, aghast. She had not typed "Q" in months. "Oh, Daddy," she whispered. The child-hood word slipped out so naturally. "Oh, Daddy, I'm *sorry.*" She sat down in her chair at the console and looked at the words on the screen. Once the "Q" had asked 10-X to check a program for errors, writing THINK AGAIN, DODO whenever there'd been a mistake in the program. It had been a joke between them. Another joke. They had shared so many jokes.

Away on the other side of the room, Karen breathed heavily in her sleep and rolled over.

"Peep, peep, peeep?"

ZUNG, UNG, UNG, sang the machinery in its niche by the dormer window.

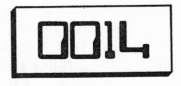

"Unnnh," groaned Karen. She raised her head and squinted at the goose.

Chloe looked right back. "Peep, peeep?"

"Geez!" Karen put her pillow over her head.

"Peep, peep, *peeep?*" Chloe abandoned the speaker and peeped to the figures in the bed.

ZUNG, UNG, UNG. ZUNG, UNG, UNG, hummed the computer, trying to keep up with the peeps.

"Okay, okay." Taylor yawned. She sat up and rubbed her eyes. Her head ached. She pulled on her jeans and an old green T-shirt that said "Greensboro Junior High." The sun was high, and she knew she'd slept later than usual. No wonder Chloe was anxious. "Zung, ung, ung," she crooned, even though Chloe had been quiet while her mistress dressed.

"Peep," said Chloe, contented.

Taylor turned off 10-X and lifted Chloe's cage from the computer top. If they went downstairs, Karen could sleep. Taylor still couldn't confess to her mother, even though she really wanted to for the first time. But she would try to be extra-nice today. "Oops," she whispered. She set Chloe's cage down and gave 10-X instructions to operate all circuits normally. She thought she'd done that, but better to be completely sure.

"Good morning," Taylor said as she plunked Chloe's cage down on the kitchen desk. "Karen's still asleep, so I came down to help with breakfast."

"Good morning yourself. We all slept late today, and I'm going to miss my appointment if I don't hurry up. You girls are on your own for a few hours. I'll be back after noon sometime."

"*What appointment?*" How could you be nice to someone who wasn't even going to *be there?*

"I'm meeting with the man I'm replacing, the librarian at Man-Trey. This was the only time he had to spend with me before I take over. He's going to explain the job and orient me to the library. I can learn a lot from him. I only wish he weren't leaving so soon." Mrs. Benson adjusted a stickpin in her lapel and looked unsure of herself.

"You'll do just *fine.* I'm not worried a bit," assured Taylor.

A surprised smile crossed Mrs. Benson's face. "Why, thank you, dear. I thought you weren't too happy about my taking this job."

"I'm just a slow adjuster," admitted Taylor, amazed to have hit on such a powerful truth. "Yeah, that's it. But you need to work and keep busy. Besides, now we can go to Florida for a vacation on your salary!"

"Best idea I've heard in years." Anne Benson tweaked a strand of dark hair into place. "I'm off then. See you sometime after noon."

Taylor had a couple of hours to play with Chloe and think before Karen woke and came downstairs. Chloe was mostly feathers now, the baby fuzz vanishing. She moved with the awkwardness that comes of knobby joints and growing feet. She was a teenager. "Like me," Taylor said slowly. "Someday we'll both be grown-up . . . and beautiful," she tacked on for reassurance. Chloe gave a delighted "wirr" as Taylor stroked her back.

Karen finally came downstairs. "Say, why don't we hunt for the high school?"

"What for?" asked Taylor.

"Because all the decent boys hang out at the high school shooting baskets and stuff. Right?"

"Okay, I guess. Where should we look?"

"Anywhere but where we were last night. I didn't see any schools then, did you?" Chloe peeped, and Taylor picked her up. The girls put her in her cage, turned on the music board, and left the house.

It took about an hour of wandering before Taylor and Karen found the schools. All three were in a row. First, a low brick building that was the elementary school; then a two-story square building, also made of red brick, that said it was Kingswood Junior High; last, another sprawling building with a white sign saying "Kingswood Consolidated High School." Around the high school was an enormous parking lot. There were five basketball hoops at one end, but no cars and no boys shooting baskets.

"Boring," said Karen. "Where is everybody?"

"Don't ask me," grumbled Taylor. "That school is huge. I'm gonna be lost there."

"Consolidated schools are always bigger. I wonder what towns all the kids are gonna come from? Besides here, I mean."

Taylor shrugged her shoulders and walked over to a window. Karen joined her at the window, and both looked into the dimness. "Look there"—Karen pointed—"boxes of books. I bet the teachers are due any day now. It's not long before school starts."

"Nope. Not long." Taylor turned away from the window and looked at the row of schools. Except for the piles of dirt stacked around each school, they looked like a movie set. No part looked as if it had just *happened.* Rigid rows of infant trees had been planted as windbreaks by each school. Construction equipment bulked like sentinels beside each pile of dirt. The site was raw—new—awful.

"Let's go back," suggested Taylor.

For lunch, Taylor broiled cheeseburgers and frozen french fries. She shook soda in a bottle in an attempt to create chocolate ice cream sodas, but most of the soda fizzed into the sink or onto the floor. It was definitely not as good as the drugstore in Greensboro, not even close.

After lunch, Taylor got out her Ouija board, but the Ouija wouldn't talk as much as she used to. There was an old Burt Reynolds movie on television, so the girls settled down to watch, bored, waiting for the afternoon to end.

"Girls," called Mrs. Benson, coming in, "did I get any phone calls while I was gone?"

"Not while we were here," answered Taylor. Burt Reynolds certainly was a hunk.

"That's funny. I left word for the power company and the builder to call today." She hung her purse on a doorknob and went to the telephone.

"You'll have to come stay with me some weekend," Karen offered. "You can meet that new boy I was telling you about. His name's Craig, did I say that? And . . . oh, I almost forgot." She hesitated. "Now don't get upset."

"Why should I get upset?" Taylor wished Karen wouldn't talk when Burt Reynolds was talking.

"Well, it's about your house. Your old house, I mean. You know how many people were looking at it?"

Taylor nodded painfully. Why not? It was a beautiful house.

"A family bought it. They have little kids, though, no older ones. They called me to baby-sit just before I left to come here. They've only been there a couple days. Their little boy is blond, with enormous brown eyes, really cute. He rides his tricycle on the porch. Just like we used to."

Taylor closed her eyes, blotting out Burt Reynolds, blotting out what Karen had said. She could see, though. See the little blond boy riding his tricycle on her porch. Counting the gray boards as she and Karen had counted them. Watching the rain on stormy days, but keeping warm and dry in the shelter of the old porch.

"You're not mad, are you, Taylor?" Karen bit her lip. "I shouldn't have told you, should I? I have such a *big mouth.*"

Taylor wanted to smile at Karen, to reassure her, but she couldn't. Now it was over. Karen lived in Greensboro, and she didn't. She lived someplace called Kingswood. A long way away.

At four o'clock Mr. Miller came to pick up Karen. Taylor waved good-bye with a sense of relief. From the car Karen called, "Don't forget to write!"

Taylor walked back into the living room and sat down. She stared at a watercolor called "Reunion," but she didn't see the picture. She could still see the little boy, though, riding up and down, up and down on the old porch in Greensboro.

"What are you doing, honey?" Mrs. Benson sounded worried.

"Just sitting."

"Let's wander down the street to the Stouts. I'll bet Stacy would like to know how Chloe's doing. We haven't seen Stacy in days."

"No, thanks. I guess I'll go upstairs and read. You go, though. It's good for you to get out."

"I wish you'd take your own advice," Taylor's mother said with a hopeful smile. "Won't you change your mind?"

"Nope." Taylor stood up and walked to the steps. "I'm fine, really. You go on, and maybe I'll come down later." She went up the steps to her room.

Mrs. Benson marched determinedly out the door. Out loud, as she slammed the door, she said, "She's not going to come later! Who does she think she's kidding?" Mrs. Benson talked to herself all the way to the Stouts'.

Taylor had been lying on her bed for only a few minutes when the telephone rang. "Oh, poop! I suppose it's that stupid builder or the power company." One step at a time she stomped down the stairs. "Hello."

"Hi. It's me. Daddy says to get out your glad rags. We're going to dinner." Stacy's excitement crackled over the phone.

"We're what?"

"Going out to dinner! And we have tickets to a play, too, in Greensboro! Just for the three of us. He said he's bored, and Mama's too tired to go anywhere. Here's Daddy."

"Good afternoon, Taylor." Mr. Stout's voice was formal and serious. Not at all like the bouncy self she'd met in the restaurant.

"Hi, Mr. Stout."

"I know this is sudden, but your mother told us that you had no plans for tonight. I have these tickets, and Mama is exhausted. She canned tomatoes all day. Now, that means *we* get a night on the town. Like Anastasia said, Taylor, put on your glad rags, and I'll be there at seven sharp." He stopped. He did not ask if it would be agreeable or if she would go. He simply stopped talking and waited.

"Uh." Taylor was nonplussed. "Uh, Mr. Stout, what are 'glad rags'?"

"Those are your best duds. A nice dress! But something you can be comfortable in. I have to shower, now, so that Stacy can have the bathroom. See you later." There was a click; then the phone buzzed dully in Taylor's ear.

When Mrs. Benson arrived home from the Stouts' house, it was nearly six o'clock. She found Taylor sitting in the living room. Taylor was still wearing her jeans and old green T-shirt.

"Mother," Taylor said coldly as Mrs. Benson came in the living room, "You went down there and fixed this up, right?"

Her mother paused. "Not really. I said Karen had come and gone, and we still had weekend left over. Only I have office material to study and you don't. Mr. Stout said,

'Wonderful, now we have somebody to use our extra play ticket.' And he sent Stacy to the phone."

"I don't believe you, and I'm not going."

"Tough! You can go get bathed and dressed this minute! We're not going to hurt the feelings of people as generous as the Stouts. *It's not a subject for debate.* Now go get ready and put a *smile* on your face!"

Taylor's ears burned. She could never remember her mother talking to her that way. Never. *Okay, madam, if that's the way you want it!*

Taylor argued with herself and called her mother names the whole time she got ready. By seven o'clock her hair was shining in dark curls over her ears and across her forehead. Her deep brown eyes snapped, but not with excitement. She was still angry. How dare they plot to make her feel better! Did they think she was three years old and too dumb to figure it out! It was stupid, that's what it was, just plain stupid.

"You look lovely," Anne Benson declared when Taylor came downstairs. "I've always thought that apricot challis was your prettiest dress."

"Thank you."

"There he is now, right on time. Remember what I said about the *smile.*" Mrs. Benson opened the door and waved to Stacy, who was sitting in the front seat of the car. Mr. Stout trotted briskly up the front walk.

"Is the second member of my harem ready?"

"She is, and I thank you again, George. Have a wonderful evening."

Gallantly George Stout took Taylor's arm and escorted her to the car. He seated her and closed the door. Very formal it was.

Except for the sound of the car motor, there was quiet in the car. Stacy and Taylor looked straight ahead, and neither one said a word. Mr. Stout couldn't stand it.

"Well, what're you ladies hungry for? I made a reservation at The Versailles Room, but if that doesn't suit, we'll go somewhere else."

"*The Versailles Room?*" Taylor's icy surface cracked.

"Wow!" said Stacy.

"Only the best. Don't want anyone saying I don't know how to entertain pretty females. There's a string quartet there this weekend, according to the *Greensboro Register.* They'll be playing some Mozart, a little Bach, and some of Haydn's quartet pieces. A rest for the mind." He sighed, with obvious anticipation.

Taylor leaned forward to look at George Stout. He was wearing a gray pin-striped suit, with a vest and sober dark tie. He liked string quartets. Were there *two* George Stouts? "When did you learn to like violins, Mr. Stout?"

"In junior high, Taylor. My father played the violin, and he made me play it. I hated it at first. Thought I'd be playing 'Twinkle, Twinkle, Little Star' till I was a grampa." He chuckled. "But by the time I got to college I wasn't too bad. They let me play in the orchestra anyway. Maybe they were desperate."

Taylor smiled at him weakly. *My stars,* as Aunt Cissy would say. *What next?* She wanted to stare at him, *hard,* to decide what he was really like. But that was rude.

"How's Chloe?" Stacy asked. "My babies are growing up so fast I can't stand it. I like 'em little."

"She's fine." Remembering Karen's distaste, Taylor added, "My friend Karen was afraid to hold her. She said Chloe would *do* something on her clothes."

"Smart friend." Mr. Stout shook his head with disgust. "I think birds dream of covering the world with you-know-what before they die. My idea of hell on earth is life in a chicken coop!"

Again Taylor was surprised, and amused. "I thought farmers liked chickens and stuff."

"Well, you see, I inherited the farm just like I inherited the violin. No choice. I majored in agriculture at college, just like everybody expected. Sometimes that's a mistake. If there's a little voice inside you saying, 'Do something else,' you'd better listen."

Stacy said quickly, "Daddy, you never told me that! I'll bet you like it better in Kingswood than on the farm, don't you?"

"Sure is more restful. I've read four books since we moved, and I'm managing five different farms. It's a whole new life, Stacy." His tone was serious. "Speaking of new life, Taylor, those diets of yours have whittled me down by four pounds already. Thanks for all that work with the computer."

The remainder of the ride into the city was a discussion of 10-X and what it could do. Taylor explained computers, and the miles flew by. Stacy insisted that Taylor define "byte" and "nybble" again, for her father's benefit. "Think of some other funny ones like that," Stacy urged.

"Well," Taylor said thoughtfully, "I'm used to the words so they aren't very funny to me, but there's 'bug.' A bug is a mistake in a program. Then there's 'debug.' That's what you do to get rid of mistakes."

As they were pulling up in front of the hotel where The Versailles Room was located, Mr. Stout asked a question. "Taylor, could you teach me to work your computer? I'm sure I could turn some of my farm management problems over to a computer. I could have it do feed orders, keep track of inventories, ration out fertilizer, things like that, couldn't I?"

"Sure, Mr. Stout. You might even want your own computer someday. You wouldn't have to *build* one, just *buy* one. But you're welcome to learn on 10-X."

George Stout escorted Stacy and Taylor into the hotel while a uniformed attendant parked the car. A black tuxedo met them at the entrance to The Versailles Room and led them to a table next to a parquet dance floor. Three more tuxedos presented menus and stepped back to lose themselves in the red velvet draperies at the side of the room.

"This menu weighs as much as I do!" exclaimed Stacy. "And I can't read it."

"See?" teased Mr. Stout. "I told you Latin wasn't spoken in Iowa. *Attendez, mademoiselles,* and Daddy Stout will read the goodies. And tonight, no counting calories. One night won't ruin our diets."

Taylor abandoned all pretense at politeness and stared openly at little round Daddy Stout. Violins, books, and now *French!* She listened as he read each item in French and translated. Each of them decided on an hors d'oeuvre, an entrée, and a dessert. Magically, as if the tuxedos at the side of the room could hear them reach a decision, the three waiters appeared. Mr. Stout ordered in French and then turned to watch as the string quartet tuned up.

Dinner and the music were an experience. Taylor and Stacy had never felt so much like royalty. Mr. Stout told hilarious stories about his troubles with animals on the farms he was managing. He explained the music that the quartet played. He poured them each a glass of pale pink wine. When dinner was over, he stood up and asked Stacy to dance. He piloted her smoothly around the parquet floor as Taylor watched in amazement. When it was her turn, she said she couldn't do the Viennese waltz.

"Of course you can." He smiled, and he was right. So well did he lead that Taylor found it easy. She had always loved dancing, and the Viennese waltz was beautiful.

"It's like living in another time, that dance," she said as they sat down at the table. Mr. Stout nodded, understanding.

"Wait till I'm thinner, you two. Then I'm going to take disco lessons if the doctor will let me. We'll have practice sessions in our rec room, and *then* we'll give the public a treat." He winked and reached for the check. "Time to go if we're going to see that play."

On weekends, from late summer through the winter, the Greensboro Repertory Theater gave two performances a night. Tonight they were to see the late performance of Agatha Christie's famous mystery play *The Mousetrap.*

"This play's been running in London for over thirty years," whispered Stacy's father as they took their seats. "I figure they have all the *bugs debugged* by now." He winked at Taylor.

Taylor smiled back and thought of her father. He had loved mysteries.

When Mr. Stout said good-night at the Benson's door, it was almost one o'clock in the morning. Taylor shook his hand awkwardly as a thank-you. Her head was so full of the surprising evening that she couldn't think of what to say. On impulse she leaned forward, and down ever so slightly, to kiss his cheek.

"I won't tell Mama," whispered Mr. Stout as he accepted the kiss.

Taylor giggled. "I'll call Stacy about Chloe's pool in a day or so. Are you sure that gravel for the pool won't cost anything?"

"Positive. I'll have it dropped off right away. Out back under the trees, right?"

Taylor nodded, they said good-night again, and she went inside. In bed, she could see the luxurious Versailles Room in her mind and hear the violins. Her father hadn't been a dancer, but he had loved music. He would have liked George Stout.

Sunday morning was almost gone before Taylor woke up. Chloe had been quieter than usual, so accustomed she was growing to her cage and  the singing computer. "It's your turn today, Chloe. We'll go play in the meadow," promised Taylor as she dressed.

Taylor spent the rest of Sunday morning telling her mother all about the fantastic evening in the city. It was a good talk, a long talk. It was the best and longest talk they'd had in many weeks. Taylor volunteered to clean the downstairs so that her mother could read the pile of information she'd brought home from Man-Trey on Saturday afternoon. Mrs. Benson accepted her offer with thanks and settled down at the kitchen table to read.

Sunday was a satisfying day. At the end of it, everyone was content. Taylor felt so noble she could hardly stand herself. She had treated her mother to a clean house and Chloe to a browse in the meadow. A television program planner way off in New York rewarded her with a Sunday evening movie she'd always wanted to see—a good end to a good day.

Monday morning at eight forty-five Mrs. Benson adjusted her blouse collar for the fifteenth time and said she was off to work. Taylor waved her good-bye with a smiling face. Her mind and heart were not smiling, however. What was she going to do all week until school started? Listlessly she set the breakfast dishes in the sink and stared out the window at the backyard. It was pale green now, grass covering the soil with determined blades.

"Hey? You in there?" Stacy called through the back screen.

"Hi!" She was glad to hear Stacy's voice.

"Did your mom go to work today?" Stacy bounced up the three steps from the back hall into the kitchen. She was wearing jeans and a top that looked like a bathing suit. "Daddy said the gravel was coming this morning, so I thought I'd come down and help you dig. It's hot, so I wore my bathing suit. I brought a spade, too."

"Yeah, it's all icky again. I'll put on my suit, too. Mother went to work just a few minutes ago. I didn't know what I was going to do all week. *Now* I know!" Taylor ran upstairs for her old bathing suit.

"Are you sure you want it that big?" Stacy and her spade sat down in the shade and watched Taylor trace an outline for the pond. "We'll be here all day."

Taylor began digging. "Whew. You're right. I'm hot already. Get the hose, and we can squirt each other to cool off."

Stacy pulled the hose out to the excavation site. "I suppose digging burns up a lot of calories."

"Digging does. Watching doesn't." Taylor leaned on her spade and grinned at Stacy.

"Myah!" Stacy made a face, but began digging.

"Where did your dad learn French? In college?" Taylor puffed as she carried a spade full of dirt to the pile she was building.

"Um-hm, and he spent a year in France after he graduated. Working with farmers there on soils, and livestock, too, I think. He says everybody thinks the ag majors are dummies."

Taylor nodded. "Yeah, it's true, they do. Especially city people. I don't know anything about farms, just what I hear."

"Daddy went back to France when I was a kindergartner. He read a paper at some big agriculture meeting. Mama went, too, but I had to stay home with my grandma." Stacy looked longingly at the hose. "How about a squirt? I'm dying."

The girls doused each other and returned to the digging. The sound of a truck interrupted them, and they leaned on their spades, panting, to watch while a pickup truck dumped a load of gravel next to the garage. The driver waved at them and drove off.

"You mean we have to cart that stuff way out here?"

"Daddy probably told him not to drive on your new grass. I can't wait to have grass, and a house, and trees of my *own.* "

"Not me. I want to live in an apartment with a skylight ... and a stereo playing in the evenings, like Whitney does. I want a neat job and fancy vacations. For a while anyway."

"You can't have lots of kids in an apartment, and I'm gonna have a whole bunch of kids. Seven or eight at the least. Mama will like that, and she can come help when I have a new one."

Taylor looked at Stacy. *"Seven or eight?* My sister Whitney, you know, the one who left all those calorie charts? Whitney says modern girls don't have to just get married and have babies. They should have careers first and *do* something with themselves."

"Fine. She can do that, but what *I'm* gonna do is get married and have a great big family! That's a career."

"Seven or eight kids would be a career all right."

Several hot hours passed as the girls talked and made Chloe's pond fit the design Taylor had scratched in the new grass. They drank a pitcherful of diet lemonade when the digging was finished, swallowing glass after glass in big, thirsty gulps. Stacy's fair skin was deep pink after all the sun, but Taylor's tan had deepened to a rich color.

Stacy proceeded to get pinker as the day progressed and the pool was lined with heavy plastic donated to the project by Mrs. Benson. Together they hauled gravel, one heavy wheelbarrow at a time. As the plastic disappeared and the gravel layer deepened, Taylor's pride grew. "It looks just like a real pond!"

"Yeah," panted Stacy. She had crept to the shade of a tree and was stretched out flat on her back.

"Let's fill it with water. It'll leak at first, right?"

Stacy nodded. "It does; then it slows down. I only have to add water about twice a week to mine. Sally and Honker and the babies think it's paradise. It's easy to make a goose happy."

"You really miss the farm, don't you?"

"Sure. But Daddy's a lot happier, and I'll get over it. I just wish school would start. I wonder where it is and what it looks like."

While the hose filled the pond, Taylor described the new schools to Stacy. "I'll show you the way Thursday or *before* if you want. It doesn't look ready, though. Mostly piles of dirt."

Stacy stood up. "That's enough water. Let's get Chloe and let her try it out. All my girl geese like it better than the boys, and they're better swimmers, too."

"Come on." Taylor grinned. "Anyway, how can you tell the difference? Are you sure Chloe's a girl?"

"Sure I'm sure. I checked her when you picked her out. Boy geese have penises, like mammals. Chloe's a girl, don't worry."

"You mean a little teeny boy goose has a . . . ?" Taylor smiled at Stacy. "I think that's hilarious. I can't help it."

"Yeah. Geese are pretty funny. I hope some kids at school figure that out and adopt some of Sally's babies when I put up my sign. Maybe, if we go early, they'll let me put up my sign before the first day."

Taylor and Stacy entered the house through the back door just as the front doorbell rang. It was the builder, his electrician, and a man in green workclothes. The green workclothes spoke.

"I'm the supervisor from the power company, miss. Here to check your wiring. May we come in?"

Checking of wiring proceeded. Stacy and Taylor drank another pitcherful of lemonade. Again the green work-clothes spoke.

"Miss Benson, please tell your mother that every single circuit is working perfectly. I'll write her a note, if you prefer, and I plan to call her on the phone." He sounded bored and looked at his watch as if he had somewhere to go. Taylor thought fast. Her mother would want proof.

"You'd better write a note."

Stacy left for home around four o'clock, after they had watched Chloe paddling happily around her pond. Mrs. Benson arrived at four-thirty and took a chair out to the new pond to see Chloe and visit with Taylor. "I read the note on my desk. *And* I talked with the supervisor from the power company. I don't see *any reason* for the wiring to act up, do you?"

"Nope," Taylor replied uncomfortably. "Sounds fine to me. They were here a long time."

"Good. Now let me tell you about my day. Taylor, I think I've been really lucky. The people are charming, absolutely charming!" Mrs. Benson went on at some length about how nice everyone at Man-Trey had been all day long. "And tomorrow night you'll meet my old friend Mr. Manfred. He's coming for dinner. He has to go back to the office, but he said he wanted to meet you, even if it was only a short visit. You'll like him."

Taylor examined her hands, dirty and calloused from digging the pond. *No,* she thought, *I won't like him. And what's he doing, coming over* here *for dinner?*

Monday evening Taylor sat at the kitchen table pretending to read a magazine. Her mother hurried to and fro, preparing a special dinner

for Tuesday night. She put a gelatin mold in the refrigerator, wrapped baking potatoes in foil, and mixed fancy ice cream parfaits, which she set in the freezer.

"Now, with a steak to grill, that should be it. Doesn't it sound *good?* I've neglected cooking for the sake of the yard or the house ever since we moved here."

Taylor nodded curtly. Certainly was a lot of work just for somebody her mother hadn't seen in years. "Guess I'll go up to bed. Digging that pond was hard work." Taylor walked out of the kitchen without another word.

"Peep, peep, peep?" greeted Chloe as Taylor came upstairs.

"Oh, shut up!" snapped Taylor.

ZUNG, UNG, UNG, soothed Mother 10-X.

Taylor undressed and got into bed. She told herself she ought to go downstairs and brush her teeth. Then she told herself to forget her teeth. She put her head under her pillow and tried to go to sleep. Sleep wouldn't come, and she knew why. She was too angry about this Will Manfred person. Who did he think he was?

Taylor decided she didn't have to be nice to him. After all, he was her mother's friend, not hers. Maybe, if he came and had a rotten time, he wouldn't come back. Of course, her father would not like that. "THINK AGAIN, DODO." Yeah, that's what he'd say. If he were here. It was a long time before Taylor fell asleep, and when she did, the pillow was wet.

After Mrs. Benson went to work the next morning, Taylor sat at the kitchen table and thought. Yes, it was wrong. Yes, it made her feel awful, and she was going to get in trouble. But she would do it anyway. She pushed her chair back and stepped quickly up the stairs before she changed her mind.

BEBOP.

HALLELUJAH! GIVE ME A JOB.

BOMB.

Then she went downstairs and packed a lunch. She took her big book on birds and put Chloe in her camping backpack. They would go to the meadow and spend the day. The whole day.

Eight hours later, at six o'clock, Taylor walked in the kitchen door. "Hi. Have a good day at work?"

Mrs. Benson hung up the telephone receiver. "I was calling Stout's to see if they knew where you were. I'll thank you to leave a note. That's always been our rule here, you know, when someone leaves the house." The ring of their doorbell interrupted her speech. "And now we have company. Run upstairs, and change clothes, please, and *remember your manners.*" Taylor's mother hurried out of the kitchen, heading for the front door.

Taylor walked upstairs, her steps tired. Yup. She was in trouble all right. She wondered whether her mother knew yet that the electricity was off. That it had been off all day, so that the parfaits were melted in the freezer and the gelatin runny in the refrigerator. As she threw her clothes on the bed and settled Chloe in her cage, she listened to the greetings below her in the living room.

"Cheers!" said a deep voice. "These are for the cook, Anne. You'd better put them in water right away. I'm afraid they're the last the florist had to offer."

So! thought Taylor as she struggled into a sundress. *He brought flowers! Brother! Was I right or was I right?*

The large voice of Will Manfred filled the little house. "Now, Anne, nothing extra. You know I have to get back to the office to work on that advertising pamphlet. Until it's finished, I'm swamped." The living-room rocker pro-

102

tested, then began to creak rhythmically.

"Don't think about it now, Will. I'll slip these flowers into water and bring you a glass of wine while I broil the steak. We're almost ready for dinner. Everything's set."

Taylor listened and wished she could stay upstairs. To walk downstairs into nothing but trouble was a dreadful prospect. But she knew there was no choice. *I don't have to go alone, though,* she thought. *I'll take Chloe with me.* She turned off the music board and tucked Chloe into her camping backpack once more.

As Taylor came downstairs, she saw her mother at the kitchen table, setting steak knives and plates for dinner. Taylor turned and went into the living room. She held her hand out and introduced herself. "How do you do? My name's Taylor. It's nice to meet you."

"Peep, peeep?" whimpered Chloe. She was hungry, and her mash was upstairs.

"What's that? A feathered friend?" Mr. Manfred stood up and peered over Taylor's shoulder at the goose. "So it is! Mmm, hmm, mmm," he crooned to Chloe.

"Peep?" Chloe examined the new voice.

"How'd you know what to do?"

"I kept geese and ducks and jaybirds and mice and you-name-it when I was a kid. Drove my folks batty. My kids have dogs and cats and a coon now. Don't know what all we'll have next week. I almost became a vet, but my grades weren't good enough. It's a tough field. So I went into business. Still rather be a vet, though." He paused. "Oh, and how do *you* do? Got so interested in your bird I forgot my manners." He grinned and held out his hand.

Solemnly Taylor shook his hand. Mr. Manfred sat down in the rocker again, and Taylor sat down on the couch. Her mother was right. Mr. Manfred was a nice man. A father. Taylor's stomach began to knot. Her head throbbed, and she wanted to throw up.

"Will?" Mrs. Benson stood in the hall doorway, fists

103

clenched at her sides. "Would you come out to the kitchen, please?"

Taylor watched him leave the room, and she prayed to die. God could just reach down and take her now. *Please, God,* she begged. Minutes passed. Then Will Manfred came back in the room.

"Put Chloe away now, Taylor. The electricity's off, so we'll run down to the shopping center and eat in the cafeteria. Hurry up." It was a voice used to giving orders.

Taylor stood up as if she were hypnotized and walked upstairs. She put Chloe in her cage and switched on the music board. Then she went downstairs and out the door. Mr. Manfred held open the door of his car, and she got inside. As they drove to the shopping center, the adults talked about the Man-Trey Company.

"I'm not hungry," Taylor said as they seated themselves in the cafeteria.

"All right. I'll put a soft drink on my tray for you," said Mr. Manfred. "You can sip that while we eat, and maybe later you'll feel like eating." He and her mother left the table and lined up to go through the maze of food choices.

Taylor drank her ginger ale while her mother and Will Manfred visited over dinner. Mr. Manfred talked about his children and the new school. Everyone, it seemed, was delighted to have Kingswood chosen as the site for the consolidated high school. It meant that Kingswood kids could walk to school and would have a better school, since the resources of four communities had been combined. Young children in the three nearby communities would stay in their hometown schools until junior high school. Then they would come to Kingswood. "Iowa's education," announced Mr. Manfred, "is something I'm proud of. And I don't know of another state that supports its state universities as we do. My years at the university were some of the best ones of my life." He turned to look at Taylor.

"Your father, Taylor, was as fine a professor as ever lived. He taught me how to *think*. That's a gift."

Taylor listened to Mr. Manfred. The ginger ale was an icy ball in her stomach. She had never felt so awful in her entire life.

At the curb in front of the Bensons' house, Mrs. Benson shook Mr. Manfred's hand as she thanked him for the dinner. "Next time, when your family is home from visiting grandparents, we'll have a dinner here. I'm eager to meet your wife, and Taylor will enjoy meeting the children. Run on, now. I know your mind is on that pamphlet. Thanks again." She waved good-bye.

Taylor walked up the sidewalk to the front steps. Mrs. Benson unlocked the door and went inside. Taylor followed her and then began to run for the bathroom. Up came the ginger ale and the undigested bologna sandwich she'd eaten for lunch.

"Wipe your face and brush your teeth, Taylor. I'll be in the living room," said Mrs. Benson.

"Now," she said when Taylor entered the living room, "sit down, and let's have it. I'm waiting."

"I didn't know he had a family," Taylor trembled.

"Mr. Manfred?"

"Yes. I thought he was coming here like, well, like a boyfriend or something. You made him sound like that."

"I didn't mean to. But what if I did? Someday I may really have one, a man who is what you call a boyfriend. Then what?"

"You would do that? With Daddy hardly dead?"

"Taylor, listen to me. I loved your father. Everybody did. But he's not here anymore. I am alone. You have made very sure that I am alone. And I resent it!"

"What do you mean? It's not my fault he died! It's not my fault you're alone!" She raised her head in anger.

"Of course, it's not your fault he died. It's no one's fault. But since that time you have pulled so far away that I haven't been able to count on you for anything. Has it ever occurred to you that *I* have a right to grieve also? That *I* might need some cheering up? I've been the rock for everyone in this family. *Good old Anne. She's tough. She* can take it." Her voice rose to a pitch Taylor had never heard. "Well, I'm *not* so almighty tough! And I'm *sick* of taking it! Particularly what you're dishing out!"

"I'm sorry." Taylor's voice was a whisper. "I guess I didn't think about you."

"You certainly didn't! You've been so wrapped up in your own misery. . . ." She stopped. "But, Taylor, you're punishing me for something *I can't help.* And I want it stopped *now.* Right now!"

"Yes, Mother."

"The power company supervisor said these homes were wired and designed to be run by a computer, if we wanted to invest in one, but I don't want any part of it! You drove Aunt Cissy out of here with that computer, didn't you?" She paused. "And tonight's dinner? All melted in the refrigerator and the stove refusing to work? You do all of that with 10-X, don't you?"

Taylor nodded. She wanted to throw up again.

"Then let me promise you something. If any of this happens again, I am taking that computer to the *junkyard!* I don't need it."

Taylor heard only one word—*junkyard.* "You wouldn't do that! Daddy and I built 10-X, and you can't destroy it. It's all I've got!"

"*It is all you have let yourself have,* Taylor. You have hidden behind that machine since the day we got here. There are plenty of kids out there. School starts in two days, and you know only one family on this street."

"How do you know there're kids here? You work all day!"

"I've been at work for only two days! I can see bicycles in driveways, even if you can't. I understand that Stacy would be too shy to meet kids since she's lived on a farm all her life, but you're not shy. You've always had lots of friends." She thought briefly. "Do you think your father would be proud of the way you're acting? Think about that, Taylor. *What would he think of all this?*"

Taylor bowed her head. Her mother was saying the things she had said to herself in the cafeteria. Her father would be disappointed, sad, angry. Most of all, he would never understand why she had treated her mother so badly. How could he, when she didn't even understand herself?

"Taylor? I don't expect you to be perfect. But I have never been so angry with anyone in my life. *This will not continue!*" She took a deep breath. "I'm going to my room now to collect myself and try to calm down. I want you to do the same thing. I'll come up later and say good-night." Mrs. Benson stood up and walked swiftly out of the room.

Taylor dragged upstairs to her bedroom. She was so tired she was dizzy. Her stomach was still heaving, threatening to erupt any minute.

"Peep, peep?" Chloe greeted Taylor with cheer.

ZUNG, UNG, UNG, answered 10-X.

Taylor walked over to the nook by the dormer window where 10-X operated the goose nursery. Wearily she slumped down into the chair in front of the console. Blank and uncomprehending of the misery in front of it, the computer screen looked out on the world.

BEBOP, Taylor keyed.

HALLELUJAH! GIVE ME A JOB.

100%. Now the house would function again.

THANK YOU. IT WAS NOTHING.

Taylor's head throbbed as she looked at the video screen. *Oh, Daddy,* she cried inside, *Mother hates me. She really does. And I've been so awful. I don't even like myself.*

Knowing it was meaningless, knowing there was no sense to the words in 10-X's computer language, Taylor keyed anyway, I HATE MYSELF.

Instantly there was a loud buzz in 10-X's circuitry. Smoke seeped out from the sides of the computer, and an acrid smell filled the air. Then the room was silent. 10-X did not hum.

"Peep, peep, peeep?"

The music board did not reply.

"Peep, peeeep, peeep?" Chloe queried again.

Silence. Taylor felt 10-X. It was warm, but it wasn't working. It wasn't even trying to work. Stiffly she stood up and walked over to her bedside table. She flicked the lamp switch. It did not come on.

I've blown the circuit to this floor, she said to herself. *And 10-X is ruined.*

"Peeep, peeep, peeeeep?"

"Zung, ung, ung," answered Taylor mechanically. It was true. She'd done it with the words she keyed in. "I hate myself" had done to 10-X just what "super" had done to the vacuum and to Aunt Cissy's curling iron.

"Pfeeep, pfeep, pfeeeep?" Chloe was shrilly insistent.

"Zung, ung, ung. Zung, ung, ung," soothed Taylor with more feeling.

"Peep, peeep?" Chloe asked, a bit calmer.

Taylor walked back toward the computer and Chloe's cage. Maybe, if Chloe ran around a while, she'd feel better. "Zung, ung, ung," she sang slowly, petting the gosling as she took her out of the cage.

Chloe rubbed her bill under Taylor's chin. "Peep." When she was put down on the rug, she stayed close to Taylor. Taylor, not knowing what else to do, sat down in the middle of the rug. Chloe climbed in her lap for a minute, then waddled off to inspect the underside of the double bed.

Mrs. Benson found Taylor sitting in the middle of the

rug when she came upstairs a few minutes later. Chloe was under the bedside table, inspecting a little pile of bird doo she had deposited on the floorboards. "Yech!" Anne Benson pointed. Taylor followed her mother's finger.

"Oh. She's not used to being out of her cage in the house. I'll clean it up." Taylor started to rise to her feet, but Mrs. Benson sat down and pulled Taylor back down next to her.

"Taylor, I'm sorry. I said some terrible things because I completely lost my temper." Anne Benson took Taylor in her arms and held her close. *"I love you,* and I'm worried sick about you."

Gradually, very gradually, the tenseness flowed out of Taylor as she sat on the floor in her mother's arms. Neither one said anything for a while; they just held each other. The heaving in Taylor's stomach subsided, and she rested quietly.

"Please, Taylor, let me come in. Don't wall me out the way you have. I can't stand it out there. It's too lonely."

Taylor nodded against the loving shoulder and slow tears dripped down her cheeks. Yes. Yes, it had been awfully lonely. "I . . . I never *thought* about what I was doing, not really. I just *did* it. And I'm sorry now. I'm awfully, awfully sorry."

"I know, I know. And it'll be better from now on. You don't have to apologize, honey. Put Chloe in her cage, and let's go downstairs. I'll make some tea to help settle your stomach."

"If you earn half the amount of 10-X's repair," Mrs. Benson called out the back door to Taylor, "I'll put up the other half. But only if 10-X is used for *peaceful* purposes, you understand."

Taylor waved good-bye to her mother and smiled. "No war. I promise. I'll be back soon to tell you how rich I'm going to be!"

Good for me, Taylor said to herself as she walked slowly down the street. *I sounded pretty hot. Getting jobs to earn allowance is nothing, right?* No sweat. *Hah! Boy, how dumb can I get?*

Chloe resting in a backpack against her back, Taylor walked all the way to the end of their street. Every now and then Taylor yawned. Chloe had spent the night in a basket next to her bed, and the regular goosely peeping had made sleep a struggle. Taylor had answered the gosling faithfully all night long, but this morning she'd been more than ready to fix Chloe a hay-bale house in the garage. Luckily the Stouts had provided the hay bales and the assurance that Chloe could begin to spend time in the garage. Except that Chloe wasn't *ready* to be alone just yet.

At the far end of King's Court, the new houses dwindled to nothing, and vacant lots stretched ahead of Taylor and Chloe. Over to the east, giant holes in the earth waited for cement blocks to create basements, for boards to build rooms above, for shingles to close them in. One street away, hammers pounded and whining saws shrilled their song, "New House, New House." More promises.

Taylor turned and looked at the house on her right. It had fluffy Priscilla curtains in the windows. A woman was sweeping the garage and humming. Two tricycles stood on the sidewalk by the front porch. Little kids then.

Taylor introduced herself to the young woman sweeping the garage. "How nice of you!" the woman said. "I'd love to get away from the twins now and then. Come inside, and I'll write down your name and number. Then you can meet the twins."

Taylor met the twins, Randy and Robbie. Randy aimed his plastic airplane and fired it with a shriek at her head. Robbie sat on the edge of his sandbox and dribbled sand into her sneakers. As Taylor waved good-bye to them, she dreaded earning money in the house with Priscilla curtains.

The worst had been first. After the twins were several houses where Taylor could earn money more enjoyably. Only a few doors from the Bensons she met a family that had four boys, one of them an eighth grader named Terry. He was more interested in the bike he was repairing than in Taylor, but he was friendly. Now they could say "hi" to each other when they met on the street.

As she walked in her own driveway, Taylor had a new idea about earning money. Maybe she could sell services on her computer. It was an exciting thought, a much better thought than sitting with Randy and Robbie. Taylor stopped for the third time and took off her tennis shoe to shake out some sand.

When Taylor told her mother about the morning, Mrs. Benson asked, "No other junior high girls on our street?"

"Nope. But. . . ." Taylor thought a minute. "You know, I really like Stacy. She's funny, and she always cheers me up. Yeah, I like her a lot."

"Good, because we're picking her and her mother up in about fifteen minutes to go shopping. Since my office is being painted, and I can't go to work, I thought we'd catch up on all our errands today. We'll get you new jeans, and then you'd better pop over to the school to ask the principal about Chloe. If I'm at work tomorrow, she can't stay alone in that garage, can she?" Mrs. Benson paused. "Oh, and another thing. Mr. Stout came by and offered to take

10-X in for a repair estimate. Wasn't that nice?"

Taylor blinked. "Mr. Stout's *awfully* nice, but *Chloe!* Do you think the principal would let me wear her to school for just a couple days? She might be all right in her house by the weekend, but not now. It's too *new.*"

At two o'clock that afternoon two new pairs of jeans met on the corner. "Boy, they're stiff! I hate new jeans," said Taylor. "Come on, the school's over this way near that other bunch of houses. I sure hope the principal understands about Chloe."

Taylor pointed as they neared the row of schools, "Look at that, Stacy! They put sod down and took away the dirt piles. It looks a lot better."

"What're all those little signs?"

Taylor walked tenderly across the new sod in front of the elementary school. "K-1" said the sign to the left of the front walk. "K-2" said the sign to the right of the walk.

"I think they're classes," Stacy suggested. "Look at the other signs. Are the classes meeting outdoors the first day or what?"

Inspection of the junior high revealed more signs in the grass. The girls walked up the front steps and into the cool air of the building. Stacy had made a poster advertising her baby geese, and she looked for a bulletin board in the hallway. From the school's office came the sound of a typewriter's staccato.

"Let's ask in here," Stacy said. "Hey?" she called as she opened the door to the office.

"Hey yourself," answered a cheerful voice from around the corner. A woman with white hair and glasses appeared. She smiled at Taylor and Stacy and nodded when she saw the poster and Taylor's backpack. "Aha! It's the goose group. Am I right?"

Taylor and Stacy smiled back. "Could I talk to the principal?" Taylor asked.

"I need to hang up this poster," Stacy said. "And what're all those little signs outside in the grass?"

"Those signs in the grass were Mr. Pomfret's idea," replied the woman. "He's our principal. Each sign represents a class. Each class, with its homeroom teacher, will be landscaping one section outside each building. Doesn't that sound like fun? We'll do that Thursday and Friday while we all get to know each other. It's a new school for everyone, you see."

Taylor and Stacy looked at one another. Decent. Very decent. The principal sounded all right.

"Now, you wanted to see Mr. Pomfret about that little goose, didn't you? Your mother phoned to say you were coming in, and Mr. Pomfret can see you now. Just go right in there." The school secretary pointed the way for Taylor.

"And *you* have to hang a poster. Follow me, and we'll put it right in the center of our main bulletin board." Stacy followed the woman out into the hall.

Five minutes later Taylor and Chloe met Stacy in the main hall. "This's gonna be okay," Stacy said approvingly as they looked around the main hall. Taylor nodded, Chloe peeped, and they all listened to teachers' voices drifting out of the separate rooms. They heard books being thumped into shelves and chalk writing teachers' names on blackboards. Tomorrow the teachers would say, "Good morning, class. My name is. . . ." Just like every fall. Only this fall, for two days only, Taylor would wear a goose to school.

That evening Mrs. Benson and Taylor entertained the Stout family. Stacy and Taylor, after visiting with the grown-ups for a while, put Chloe in her hay-bale house and went upstairs to Taylor's room to talk. It was the first time Taylor had really looked at her room since Mr. Stout had taken 10-X away.

Taylor flipped on the switch that turned on her over-head light, restored to power by the builder's electrician. Her eyes were drawn to the niche made by the dormer window where 10-X had stood since the day they'd moved in. Now the dormer nook was bare. On the floor lay all of the music board equipment. Slowly Taylor walked over to the window. She could see a streetlamp across the way, and the branches of the trees bending in the wind.

"What's the matter?" Stacy had come over to the dormer.

"10-X always sits here. It's funny with it gone."

"But Daddy said tonight it'd only be a week, remember?"

"Yeah, and that's good. But it's weird with it gone. 10-X has been in my room since I was ten and a half."

"Ten? Is that why you named him 10-X?" Stacy sat down on the rug and looked up at Taylor.

"Really my father named it. He said I was ten and our computer was an unknown quantity, an X, so we'd put our numbers together, sort of. We'd see, he said, what a ten and an X could do."

"I'm beginning to feel like I know him," Stacy said. "I'm sorry. I shouldn't have said that. You're trying to forget him, and here I go again."

Taylor joined Stacy on the rug. She put a determined smile on her face. "No. It's all right. I don't want to forget. I just want it to be easier to remember, that's all." She made herself look right at Stacy as she spoke. She made the smile stay in place.

"Yeah, but it's gonna take awhile. I'm glad school's starting. That'll give us lots to think about. You don't need 10-X now anyway. Except for my menus, you haven't needed him since you got here, have you?"

Taylor looked at her lap and then at Stacy. "Let me show you something." She went over to her bed and reached under the mattress. "Read this," she said, hand-ing her the note pad where she had recorded 10-X's control of all the circuits in the house.

While Stacy read the code in the note pad, Taylor gazed out the window. The tops of the old trees swayed back and forth in autumn's dance as she watched. Yes, the trees on King's Court were nice. That was what was *still* wrong with the schools and many of the new houses. No big trees. She was going to vote for lots of trees when the eighth grade planned its landscaping for the junior high. Big trees, right away.

"Does it work? Did you *do* it, Taylor??"

"Hmmm? Oh, yeah. It works. Or it did. I'm not exactly sure how it happened, but it wasn't *supposed* to happen. At first, I thought it was a glitch." Taylor began to tell Stacy how she had discovered that 10-X *could* control the circuits at 4 King's Court. Before long she was telling the whole story.

"And, Stacy, these houses *do* have special wiring. It's all set up here for people who have home computers. Mother found out all about it from the builder."

"I don't get it," said Stacy, shaking her head.

"Mother said it was because some of the first owners here in Kingswood wanted to computerize their appliances and stuff, so they had the builder put special switches in when he was doing the wiring. It didn't cost much extra, so he did it for all the houses, and then he could say how really modern they were."

"It's better than the farm," Stacy said. "We blew fuses there all the time."

"Yeah, we did, too, in our old house. But these houses are a single circuit so a computer can connect and disconnect and make circuits where they're needed. 10-X shouldn't have been able to mess up the regular setup here, of course, but I hooked up two hot lines by mistake and overloaded the circuit. Mother said the builder and his electrician are having a fit."

"Okay," said Stacy, "but what messed up 10-X if he could control the circuits?"

"I keyed some combination of letters that overloaded the circuit, and 10-X was on that circuit."

"And he revolted!"

"Computers can't do that!"

"This one did. He up and quit. You must have told him something that he didn't like."

Gradually a smile spread across Taylor's face. She nodded. "Okay, so it revolted. And now I have to be Chloe's mother. Do you know how much sleep I *didn't* get last night?"

"I'll bet." Stacy giggled. "She'll be all right in the garage anytime now. It's better for you to be her mother anyhow, better than a machine. Machines can't be mothers."

"Anastasia??" Mrs. Stout's voice fluted up the stairway. "Time for bed. School starts early in the morning."

Stacy looked at her watch. "I knew it! Nine o'clock. When I'm twenty, they'll be reminding me to brush my teeth!" She hollered, "Coming, Mama!"

Taylor went downstairs with Stacy to say good-night to the Stout family. Stacy promised to wait on the corner in the morning so that the two could walk to school together.

"Taylor, I have an idea for you," offered George Stout. He paused, holding the door open.

"George Stout, shut that door if you're going to talk. You're letting in all the mosquitoes in the county." Mama looked at him as she'd look at a kindergartner.

Mr. Stout shut the door. "Yes, Mama. Now, Taylor, if you'd let me pay for the repair of 10-X, I could take it out in computer lessons. An exchange, you see?"

"I can't do that, Mr. Stout. It wouldn't be right. But if Mother says it's okay, I'd pay you back for the repair. Every penny."

Mrs. Benson agreed, the door opened, and this time

three Stouts went out. Taylor and her mother waved good-bye and stood watching through the screen as they walked away into the night. "How lucky we are," Anne Benson said. "I'm so glad they left their farm."

"Me, too. I wonder which memory chips are lost? Mr. Stout said the repair shop said that was what shorted out. That, and some of the wires that were the memory bus."

"Whatever it is, Taylor, you can put back all that you need. You'll need extra memory for school this fall any-way, right? And now we'd better get ready for bed. I'll be going to work tomorrow since the painting's almost finished, and you have school, even if it's only a half-day orientation. Get Chloe, dear, and we'll all turn in for the night."

Chloe met Taylor in the garage with a series of de-lighted "peeps." All the way upstairs to Taylor's room, she rubbed her beak under Taylor's chin and emitted little "wirrs."

"I *am* a better mother than 10-X," Taylor told her when they both were in their beds for the night. "But it's a tough job."

Taylor lay in bed and listened to Chloe "wirring" her-self to sleep. Tomorrow would be the first day in the new school. The wind rustled branches against her dormer window, and she turned her head to watch the tree's shadow play on the wall. With 10-X and Chloe's cage in the way, the tree had not cast its shadow before. Taylor fell asleep watching the tree make designs in the moon-light on her wall.

Stacy was waiting on the cor-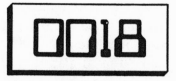
ner next morning, just as
they had planned. Taylor adjusted Chloe in her backpack
and waved at Stacy as she
hurried down the street. Taylor saw that Stacy was wearing a blue headband and her new jeans. *She looks just right
for fourth grade,* Taylor thought with amusement.

"Do you have lots of grass in there?" Stacy pointed to
the backpack. "It's going to be a long time before she can
get out of that thing. You'll be covered with doo-doo if
there isn't lots of grass."

Taylor sighed. "Stacy, that's not a cheerful subject to
start the day! Anyway, I'm getting sick of wearing her
everywhere I go. I feel like I smell of goose."

"Peep, peep?"

"Zung, ung, ung," answered Taylor.

"Don't pick on Chloe. She's gonna be the best conversation maker ever born."

Taylor shot an admiring glance at Stacy bouncing along
beside her. Stacy was very smart.

"What're you going to do with 10-X when you get him
back? Besides teaching Daddy to work him?"

"I'll put my world history questions in memory to quiz
me before tests. And it can check my math homework and
ask more questions for earth science. I'd like to computerize some of the appliances in the house, too, or . . . or lock
the garage door," she added hesitantly, remembering
plans from the past.

"Anything else? It seems like he can do a lot."

"That's what I like about it. I've been thinking," Taylor
began slowly, "about trying to earn money with 10-X
instead of baby-sitting. Mowing lawns is okay, but baby-
sitting stinks. Did I tell you about Randy and Robbie?"

Stacy grinned. "You leave them to *me.* What could you
do to earn money with 10-X?"

"Remember all those little stores we saw yesterday in Kingswood Plaza? What if 10-X could keep their records, their inventories, or do their mailing lists? Things like that. How old do you think I look?"

"Not old enough." Stacy shook her head. "But it's dumb not to try, I guess. Tell them you're fifteen. You look fifteen."

"Peep, peeep?"

"Zung, ung, ung," Taylor replied automatically.

"There they are," Stacy said as they rounded the last corner. "Wow! Are we late? Look at all those kids!"

There on the open plain, the Kingswood school system reared its triple head. Elementary, junior high, high school. The rows of baby pines and poplars that would grow into windbreaks and snow barriers were dwarfed by the students milling about, all of them waiting for the doors to open.

"I can hardly wait," muttered Taylor. "They'll hear me talking to Chloe and think I'm a nerd right away."

"Tell them you're speaking Urdu. That'll get 'em." Stacy and Taylor stood apart from the groups of chattering teenagers in front of the junior high. They watched as girls or boys were welcomed into little bunches that knew each other and were comfortable. Some of the groups looked their way, but not for long. A few students sat alone on the steps in front of the school. They tried not to look anywhere in particular. Taylor wondered if they, too, were from the new housing development.

"Peep, peep, peep?"

"Zung, ung, ung," whispered Taylor.

"What's that you said?" It was a tall boy with light brown hair. He carried a notebook plastered with basketball pictures.

"I said 'Zung, ung, ung.' It's Urdu." Taylor kept a straight face.

"Oh, yeah? What's your name? You live here in Kingswood?" He grinned, waiting to be let in on the joke this tall girl had pulled on him.

"I'm Taylor Benson. This is my friend Stacy. We both live here in Kingswood. Where do you live?"

"Hi." The boy bobbed his head in Stacy's direction and looked back at Taylor. "We'll be living here pretty soon, too. My dad's got a job at the packing plant. He says we can't afford to farm anymore. He's going broke buying equipment. We move in about a month. Till then I ride the bus with the kids from Remford."

"Do you have a name?" Stacy looked up at the newcomer.

"Sorry. It's Clark. Clark Olson. I'm from Rockwell City." He took a dramatic pose, throwing his arms out wide. "The Golden Buckle of the Corn Belt!" He dropped his arms and grinned at both girls.

Taylor grinned back. She was planning to ask him about the basketballs on his notebook when Chloe piped up. "Peep, peeep?"

"I *did* hear a peep-peeep!" Clark saw Stacy's eyes fixed on the backpack. "What've you got?" He walked around Taylor and looked in the backpack.

"Zung, ung, ung," Taylor said with a sigh. She hoped Stacy was right about Chloe. Clark Olson was awfully nice.

"Okay, why're you wearing a goose?" The grin was wider than ever.

"It's a long story." Taylor returned his grin.

"Are you gonna tell me or not?" He cocked his head to one side. By now there was a small crowd around Taylor, Stacy, and Clark.

"Hey, Olson, what's in the pack?"

"Yeah, who're your new friends, Olson?" The questions went on and on. Clark introduced Taylor and Stacy to his friends from Remford who had ridden on the bus with him. He was the only student from Rockwell City, but because he was a junior high basketball player, he knew many kids from neighboring towns. Clark said he was thinking of taking Latin in ninth grade. Stacy launched into her lecture about the joys of Latin just as the bell rang. The doors opened, and the tide swept through the opening into the auditorium.

A man wearing glasses, with about five hairs on his head, pounded a gavel on the rostrum up on the stage at the front of the auditorium. "Attention! Students? Let me point to the class sections," he shouted.

Eventually each class was seated in the proper section. Taylor looked around and guessed there were about ninety eighth graders. Not too bad. Now she knew Clark and Stacy, and she could say hello to the boy named Terry from her street—*if* she ever saw him.

The person wearing glasses and five hairs pounded the gavel again. "Quiet, please! *Quiet,* please!" He looked around the auditorium, frowning slightly. "That's better. *Now,* we can get down to business. My name is Mr. Pomfret, and I'm your new principal." He paused and shuffled some papers on the rostrum.

"Peep, peep, peeeep?" chirped Chloe in her most piercing tone. Taylor's shoulders drooped, and she scrunched down low in her seat.

"You have to be quiet too, you silly goose," said Mr. Pomfret, looking right at Taylor. "One announcement before we begin. One of our new students is named Chloe Benson. She's young, but we have great hopes for her. She's a goose, actually, in the eighth grade. Her foster mother happens to be with her today, and she's new, too. Taylor, why don't you come up here and let us meet Chloe?"

The auditorium became one giant eye peering around to find the goose student and her eighth-grade mother. Taylor turned exactly the shade of red she hated, but Stacy sat tall and looked proud. "What a wonderful ad for my babies," she whispered as Taylor slid past her out of the row of seats. Clark clapped loudly and saluted Taylor as she walked up the aisle to the stage.

"Nice to see you again, Taylor," said Mr. Pomfret. He held out his hand, and he and Taylor shook hands. "Now let's *all* see that goose." He reached into the backpack and took out Chloe. Gently he raised her above his head and held her there for everyone to see. Chloe looked around, peeped softly, and laid a pile of doo-doo in his hands. A dreadful look washed over his face as he lowered his hands and passed Chloe back to Taylor.

"Oh, Mr. Pomfret, I . . . I. . . ." Taylor chewed her lip.

When the students saw Mr. Pomfret take out his handkerchief and gingerly wipe his hands, they understood why he'd made a face. The laughter in the auditorium swelled as one person after another learned that Chloe had messed on Mr. Pomfret. Silence was a long time coming.

Order restored, the introductions began. All of the teachers stood up, gave their names and their room numbers, and then told something about themselves. Taylor and Stacy wrote everything in their new notebooks. Subjects had been selected by mail during the summer. Now the schedules for each student were passed out.

"I have to start each day with *world history,*" Taylor wailed. But she had liked the looks and the words of the world history teacher. "Look, Stacy, we have gym and English and lunch together."

The gavel pounded again. "Students, attention, please! The homeroom teachers are going to read the list of their students. Would you stand up as your name is called and leave the auditorium with your homeroom teacher?" Names were called, and groups of students departed. Stacy and Clark left together for the same homeroom. Taylor's name was called, and then Terry's. *At least there's somebody,* she thought. They filed out to their homeroom, with everyone looking around at the new building. Another year, another first day at school, was officially begun.

"My homeroom teacher's my English teacher," Taylor told Stacy on the way home. "And there are two girls in my class who used to live in Greensboro! One of them, Andrea, is really nice. We all had to stand up and tell about ourselves. Andrea said she was going to call you about a goose. Do I get a commission for palming off one of your geese?"

"Ho-ho. You can come for Thanksgiving dinner. Roast goose. Supposed to be very posh and expensive. How's that for a commission?"

"I will *never* eat goose!" Taylor declared. "Stacy, we ought to go somewhere this afternoon, and I can put Chloe in the garage. She's only got a few days to get used to being there alone. Mr. Pomfret stopped me in the hall to remind me that I could wear her tomorrow when we plan our landscaping, but no more after that."

"I like Mr. Pomfret. He's nice," Stacy said. "Most principals would've had a fit about her pooping on him like that. I'll have to ask Mama about going somewhere, but if she says yes, we ought to bike down to the shopping center and you could ask some of those little stores about doing their work on 10-X."

"Yeah! How far is it do you think?"

"About three miles, Daddy said. It'd be good for losing weight. Clark Olson doesn't know it yet, but he's a *marked man.*" Stacy's round little chin jutted out, and she wore her fierce, determined look.

Taylor smiled and nodded. Stacy was right. Clark didn't have a chance. "I'll have to talk to my mother first. She's going to call from work. Then I'll call you." The girls parted at Stacy's corner, and Taylor went home to put Chloe in her hay-bale house for the afternoon. Chloe peeped once and turned to her bowl of food.

123

When the phone rang, Taylor was ready. She had smoothed her hair into a tiny bun because it made her look older. The stores would want her to look old. "Hi. Is your office all painted?" she asked.

"Yes, it's a lovely shade of aquamarine. How was your morning?"

"Well, I met a lot of kids. Two girls in my homeroom used to live in Greensboro. My homeroom teacher's my English teacher, and he believes in *homework*. He said something about reading a book a week. Everybody wanted to hold Chloe, and I think Andrea is going to get a goose from Stacy. The principal, Mr. Pomfret, made Chloe and me get up on the stage in front of the whole school, and he held Chloe up so everybody could see her. She pooped in his hands, and he didn't get mad. Isn't that funny?

"And Stacy's in love with a boy named Clark Olson. Is it okay with you if Stacy and I bike to the shopping center?"

Taylor listened while her mother gave permission for a trip to the shopping center. Then, like an unexpected present, she got a wonderful idea. "Mother? I'm working on a surprise for you, okay? I can't do it now. Pretty soon, though, okay? See you at dinner."

"She's kicking me out!" protested Daddy Stout in mock anger. His arms were loaded with computer manuals.

"That's right, she is." Taylor's mother laughed. Mrs. Benson was watching from the living-room couch where she had settled down with a book.

"That's right, I am." Taylor smiled, her hand in the air waving good-bye. "You never want to *quit,* Mr. Stout, and it's after nine o'clock! And I'm tired. Besides, we can't do any more of your work until we get another floppy for storage. 10-X has just run out of space!" Again she made shooing motions toward the door with her hands.

Difficult as it was for him, George Stout turned serious. "Taylor, do you know how much of a help you've been? I've saved every one of my customers money in the past weeks—every one of them! And it can only get better, my dear. I may have to get one of these gadgets myself." The perennial smile decorated his face once more. "And now I'm really going. Mama says I'm a terrible pest." He waved good-bye to Mrs. Benson, blew a kiss to Taylor, and was gone.

Taylor locked the door behind their neighbor. "Mother," she said, "I'm not really tired, but Mr. Stout loses all track of time! I have your surprise ready, and I want to do it *now.* Remember? I didn't think it would take this long, but it's finally ready. Can you come upstairs for a few minutes?"

"Of course. I love surprises, as you know." She smiled as she put her book aside and followed Taylor up the stairs.

"Okay," said Taylor when they were in her room. "You sit over there on the bed. Just pile those books on the floor."

Mrs. Benson looked around the second story of their

new house and groaned. "Taylor! Isn't it embarrassing to have someone in your room when it looks like this?"

"Sorta, but Mr. Stout and Stacy understand. They know I've been working on the surprise, and Mr. Stout's work, and my homework, and . . . and so I'm behind! But now I can clean up—now that this program is finally ready." Taylor was busy working as she talked, hooking up the music board and its speaker.

"Ready?" Taylor stood in front of 10-X.

Mrs. Benson nodded and folded her hands in her lap. Taylor keyed in her password and quickly followed it with more instructions. Watching her mother, she sat down in her chair to listen.

And that was how Beethoven came to 4 King's Court. The well-loved strains of "Für Elise," played by the computer and its music board, filled Taylor's bedroom. It was not like the original, not a piano sound, but a thing of itself. This music had its own originality, its own beauty. The refrain repeated, unmistakably Beethoven, distinct, and memorable. Too soon the tones faded away. There remained the low hum of 10-X, a pale sound, a reminder.

Taylor's mother spoke, her voice barely rising above the hum of the computer. "How could you know? It's my old favorite." She closed her eyes.

"I didn't. Daddy wrote this program last . . . last May. We almost finished it that afternoon . . . before the girls came." It was too hard to say "before he died."

Mrs. Benson sighed and blinked her eyes, then wiped away the tears. "It's lovely," she managed. "But it hurts."

Taylor left her chair and sat down beside her mother on the bed. "I didn't mean for it to hurt. It was *his* surprise, really. I just finished what he started. When 10-X came back, I thought I would never use the Beethoven program. I wanted to tear it up and throw it away. But I couldn't. I tried, and I couldn't do it. He said it was the best surprise idea he'd ever had, so I couldn't just throw it away."

Mrs. Benson kissed Taylor on the forehead. "Of course not, sweetheart. But I was thinking of *you*, too. Wasn't it awfully hard to work with that program? And when did you test it so that I didn't hear?"

"When you were at work or having coffee with Mrs. Stout. That's why it took so long. I cried every time at first, but it got better. The more I listened to it, the better I felt. Do you want to hear it again?" She paused. "It's like the old piano bench we gave Whitney for her apartment. I had always sat on it with Father, to work with 10-X, you know. And at first I hated my chair, but now I hardly ever think about it."

So, once again, Beethoven's melody poured out while Anne and Taylor Benson listened and thought. "It's very different," said Mrs. Benson, "yet it's the same. And you're right. It was a little easier the second time." She smiled, without tears.

"We don't have to listen to it again, if you'd rather not," offered Taylor.

"No, it will get easier, as you said. Perhaps some evening when the Stouts are here, we could play it for them." She kissed Taylor again and stood up. "And now it *is* late, and you'd better get to bed." She went to the stairs. "And thank you. Maybe I didn't seem grateful at first, but that was a very special present."

Taylor was too keyed up to sleep, and although it was late, she straightened her room. Chloe, bedded down in the garage, wasn't there for company, but Taylor's mind was occupied with other thoughts. The new school was hard, and there was a great deal of homework, but it was fun just the same. Everyone was friendly. If she wanted to meet someone new and felt shy about it, all she had to do was ask Stacy to introduce her. In some way that Taylor didn't understand, Stacy had managed to meet absolutely everybody!

Taylor smiled as she hung up her clothes. She usually smiled when she thought about Stacy. Just that afternoon Stacy had said, out of the blue, "You *will* be their aunt, won't you? Their Aunt Taylor?"

"Whose aunt?"

"All my kids, of course. All kids have to have an aunt, and so you can be their aunt, right?"

"I hope I have a good job so I can afford to buy *all those presents,*" Taylor had joked.

"Oh, you will. I'm *sure* of that."

Taylor slipped an old, soft nightgown over her head and fluffed up her pillow. She snapped off the light, pushed her spread off the end of the bed, and pulled up the covers. Even without the light, her room was fairly bright. An autumn moon glistened in through the dormer windows on the far side of her room. Above the bulk that was 10-X, a tree's shadow was thrown on the opposite wall. It was only the young top of a tree, and Taylor thought it looked funny, growing out of 10-X that way.

The treetop seemed to thrust upward from the square, solid base and become a separate being. Patterned on the wall, its shadow swayed in varied designs while Taylor watched. *That's* my *tree,* she said to herself.

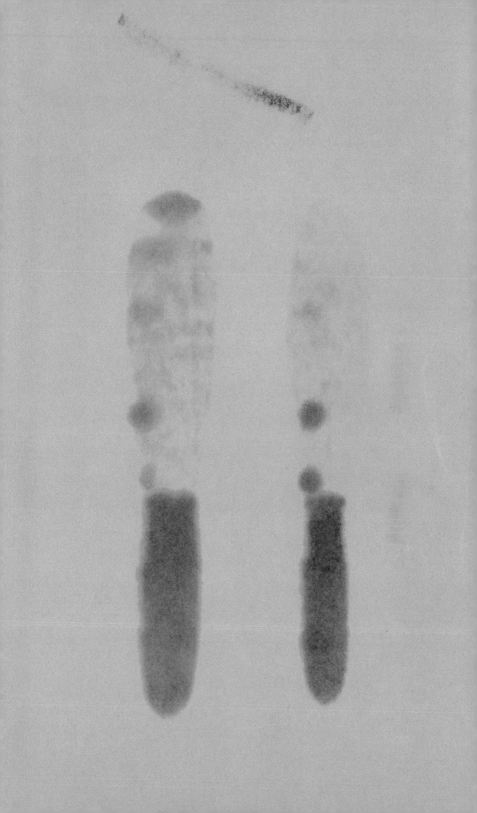

J Do c 1
Carris, Joan Davenport.
The revolt of 10-X.

8.00